Heather Allison lives in Houston, Texas. As well as being one of our favorite contributors to the Romance line, Heather also writes as Heather MacAllister for Harlequin Temptation.

Of **The Santa Sleuth**:
"The characters are a delight, and the plot will leave you in stitches. Altogether…one romance you won't want to miss!" —*Affaire de Coeur*

"a fun romp…" —*Romantic Times*

"I had trouble putting this book down… Now, I just need to read all of Heather's other books!" —*Happily Ever After*

Of **Undercover Lover**:
"4 1/2 ★'s… A fast-paced, adventurous storyline with true-to-life characters…" —*Romantic Times*

Of **Jilt Trip**:
"…With frolicking love and laughter, the talented Heather MacAllister tantalizes us with ever spiraling peaks of voluptuous magic…" —*Romantic Times*

Look out in July for Heather's next **Harlequin Romance** (#3466), **His Cinderella Bride**:

Rose Franklin was fed up with kissing frogs—she wanted Prince Charming. And then she found Duncan Burke's personal organizer and discovered the perfect man—on paper at least. All she needed to do was become the kind of woman who would fit right into Duncan's life and his social planner!

Dear Reader,

Welcome to our exciting showcase series for 1997!

SIMPLY THE BEST

*Authors you'll treasure,
books you'll want to keep!*

Harlequin Romance books just keep getting better—
and we enjoy bringing you the best choice of wonderful
romance novels each month. Now, for a whole year,
we'll be highlighting a particular author in our monthly
selections—a specially chosen title we know you're
going to want to enjoy, again and again....

This month it's the turn of Heather Allison and *Marry Me*,
a special Valentine romance. Our **Simply the Best** title
for March will be (#3448) *Getting Over Harry* by the one
and only Renee Roszel!

Happy reading!

The Editors

Marry Me
Heather Allison

Harlequin Books

TORONTO • NEW YORK • LONDON
AMSTERDAM • PARIS • SYDNEY • HAMBURG
STOCKHOLM • ATHENS • TOKYO • MILAN
MADRID • WARSAW • BUDAPEST • AUCKLAND

In memory of
Karen Lacefield Bachran

ISBN 0-373-03445-8

MARRY ME

First North American Publication 1997.

Copyright © 1997 by Heather MacAllister.

CHAPTER ONE

TONY Domenico, confirmed pragmatist, never imagined that he'd make a large part of his living by peddling romantic fluff. First-rate romantic fluff, but fluff just the same.

Moving the telephone to the edge of his desk so the cord would stretch far enough, he leaned back in his chair. "Yes, 'Hartson Flowers' will be taping a Valentine's special this year. We're in preproduction now."

Tony listened with satisfaction as the executive producer of yet another television station optioned the rights to broadcast the show—rights that were selling for more this year than last. The man didn't even quibble at the price increase and Tony half wished he'd asked for more money.

Hanging up the telephone, he entered the appropriate data into his computer before propping his feet on his desk and contemplating the water stain on the corner ceiling tile in his office.

With this latest sale of the "Hartson Flowers" Valentine special, he'd reached the break-even point and it was still early January. He hadn't even started marketing the thing properly yet. Every station that picked it up from here on out represented profit. Pure and much-needed profit.

Life was good.

Tony allowed himself to engage in a little fantasy spending, something he rarely did. He'd increase the budget on the show, naturally. Alicia and Georgia, the "Hartson Flowers" producers, deserved it. But now, maybe he could throw a little extra money to the "Storyteller's Hour", a quiet children's show that he'd been pushing for the past eighteen months without much success. The sets were cheesy and he knew it. Maybe some refurbishing would result in more stations picking up the show. It wasn't a good sign when no television station in Houston, Texas—Domenico Cable Productions' home market—carried it.

And the "Skinny Gourmet" show was on such a tight budget that they couldn't afford to make the recipes twice so they could continue taping. Taping had to stop while the food actually baked or cooked or froze or whatever.

And maybe, just maybe, he'd replace that ceiling tile.

Tony was tired of skimping because funds were tight. He was tired of asking creative people to scale down their visions or to work with barely adequate sets and props. And he was really tired of being a stepping stone, of losing promising shows to production companies who could give them bigger budgets. He wanted to attract and retain more top-quality shows like "Hartson Flowers". He wanted to be able to give newcomers a chance to develop an audience. He wanted—

There was a tap on his open door. "Tony?" A sultry brunette appeared in the doorway. "Could we talk to you for a minute?"

We? "Sure, Georgia." Hastily dropping his feet to the floor, Tony stood and waved in Georgia

Flowers. Alicia Hartson followed her and Tony braced himself.

It wasn't often that he spoke to them together. Usually he dealt with Georgia, though Alicia was the budget-and-visionary half of the team. He and Alicia didn't get along. Her unrelieved perkiness irritated him and he found her ideas wildly impractical and usually expensive. And her opinion of him, as she'd said in one memorable clash, was that he was a stingy, unimaginative bean counter.

Ever since, they'd communicated through Georgia.

Georgia was a people person and excelled at interviewing and digging up stories to go with Alicia's ideas. She also excelled at convincing Tony and Alicia to see eye to eye. Only when Alicia and Georgia wanted to try something controversial or expensive did they double-team him like this. He wondered what it was this time.

Since there were only two chairs in Tony's office, he swiveled his desk chair around and seated Georgia, who was pregnant. Hugely pregnant, but Tony refused to dwell on her impending maternity leave. His top priority was getting the Valentine special in the can.

Alicia slipped into the other chair and Tony propped a hip on the corner of his desk.

" 'Hartson Flowers' just cracked another market this morning," he told them, "and I've signed up two more stations for the Valentine special."

Alicia and Georgia exchanged glances.

Tony felt his earlier good mood evaporate. He relied heavily on his instincts and his instincts told him there was trouble ahead.

Georgia spoke. "We've run into a little snag."

"Now, Georgia, don't call it that." Alicia beamed a huge television smile. "I think it's wonderful!"

Bingo. His instincts were never wrong. And people called it indigestion. "What's the problem?"

"Oh, it's not a problem," drawled Georgia, a Southern belle who'd never lost her accent. "You do know that I'm pregnant." She gestured down at her basketball-size lap.

Tony had been watching her rapidly expanding waistline with alarm. The baby wasn't due for weeks. By March, "Hartson Flowers" would have to shoot with a wide-angle lens.

"This information does not come as a complete surprise to me," he said as neutrally as possible. "You did send me a memo and there've been several segments on your quest for maternity clothing."

"So you do watch the show?" Alicia asked.

His gaze met her cool blue one. She didn't think much of him, did she? "Yes. I wouldn't market a product I haven't reviewed." He struggled for something complimentary to say. Though the content didn't personally appeal to him, the show certainly had its fans. "You're doing well in the new markets."

"We've had good viewer feedback on the maternity segments," Alicia commented with an answering nod from Georgia.

Tony knew this. He knew their market share in each area in which "Hartson Flowers" was broadcast. That was his job. So what did they want now?

A horrible thought occurred to him. *Please do not ask me to allow "Hartson Flowers" to film the birth. Please.*

"We'd like to capitalize on the maternity angle," Alicia continued.

Tony eyed her warily.

"To do that, we'll have to make some adjustments to the show's format."

"Now isn't the time to tinker with success," Tony warned.

"We don't have a choice. Tell him, Georgia."

"Oh, Alicia, you're scaring him." Georgia turned her sultry smile on him. "I just found out that I'm having twins!"

"Congratulations." Two babies for one maternity leave. "That's very efficient of you, Georgia."

Alicia shot him a look.

Georgia continued, "Well, I'm relieved, I can tell you. Here I am as big as a house already..." She trailed off with a soft laugh.

The pause was Tony's cue to say something flattering, but what? She wasn't as big as a house, she was as big as an entire condominium. "All for a good cause," he said lamely.

The corner of Alicia's mouth twitched.

Georgia turned her smile down a few watts. "But apparently I'm not big enough. The babies need to grow and the doctor is afraid I might go into labor too early. That happens with twins sometimes. So, I'm to stay in bed for the rest of my time."

Tony managed to absorb the news without flinching. "That's the snag, right?"

"As I said," Alicia broke in, "we'll have to make some adjustments."

Adjustments? Who was she kidding? Losing half the "Hartson Flowers" team was a catastrophe. "Bed rest right away...or after the Valentine special?" Tony kept his voice even.

"Immediately," Alicia told him with a stern look.

Tony fired one right back at her. Mention babies and women always went to mush and forgot about everything else. *Somebody* had to look out for the bottom line in this situation. Obviously, he was going to be that somebody.

"Yes, I'm afraid I'm abandoning poor Alicia." Georgia touched her on the arm.

"Nonsense! You're not abandoning me!" Alicia bubbled. "You're going on maternity leave. Now *that's* romantic and 'Hartson Flowers' has always promoted romance."

Tony knew that last bit was a subtle message to him.

"You're being so sweet about this," Georgia murmured.

Implying that Tony wasn't. Well, he didn't feel particularly sweet at the moment. "Your health and the health of your children are what's important." He said it to remind himself as much as to reassure Georgia.

Alicia's expression thawed slightly. "You see?" she said. "I told you he'd understand."

Tony understood, all right. He understood that he should never have allowed himself to daydream about spending the extra money. Dreaming was a waste of time. Hadn't that been proven to him over and over again?

"And it's not like you're going to be doing nothing," Alicia continued to reassure Georgia.

Tony half listened while he tried to think of some way to salvage the Valentine special.

"Just think, we can still follow your pregnancy. You aren't the first woman who's been confined to bed. You know..." Alicia bit her lip. "We wanted to explore the computer on-line services. You can do that from your bed."

Georgia perked up. "And we can do a feature on bed jackets and lounging clothes!"

"Book reviews."

"Videos."

"How about a world-at-your-fingertips series of all the services you can order over the telephone?"

"Once I figure out how!" Georgia laughed and opened her notebook.

The women continued to talk as though Tony wasn't in the room. He listened, admiring the way the ideas poured out of them and the way they analyzed them for potential, discarding immediately the ones they felt wouldn't work.

Tony was getting an impromptu demonstration of how "Hartson Flowers" came to be his most popular show. The two women shared a special chemistry, along with their individual talents. That they enjoyed what they did was evident, along with their love of the mushy human interest stories that had become their trademark. They dealt in fluff, but they weren't fluffbrains. Just overly optimistic at times.

If ever there was an example of making lemonade out of lemons, this was it. Both women had come into his office carrying notebooks and both were now scribbling as fast as they talked.

Tony could hardly make out what they were saying, since their sentences had degenerated into a verbal shorthand. Alicia's notes were filled with facts and figures, Georgia's with names and companies.

He shook his head. They were good. Really good. Too good to stay with Domenico Cable Productions much longer.

Tony's company wasn't a major syndicator, and "Hartson Flowers" was ready for the big time. With the annual Valentine specials, they'd attracted enough attention to their show that Tony knew he could sell the series to a major network. It would be quite a coup for all of them.

And if he didn't sell the show soon, then someone else would copy the format with a bigger staff, a bigger budget and a better set. It was surprising that it hadn't already been done.

He broke into their planning session. "This all sounds great. You know I'll support you in whatever you decide."

"We know." Alicia closed her notebook. "You always have."

She smiled and for a moment Tony's attention was caught by the rare warmth and approval in her blue eyes. Normally, he didn't care whether or not people approved of him and wondered at the small satisfaction he felt now.

Alicia was an attractive woman, not stunning like Georgia with her beauty-contestant good looks, but pretty. Cute, he supposed. Perky and blond. But not his type, even if they didn't already dislike one another. She was much too talkative for him. He liked quiet, peaceful women, not women who charged the air when they entered a room.

He cleared his throat. "Since neither of you has mentioned the Valentine special, I suppose I'm going to have to."

Alicia looked down at her hands before meeting his gaze. "With Georgia out and a three-week shooting schedule, I don't see how we can produce it this year."

"We thought about featuring one couple here in Houston either proposing or getting married, and some romantic date ideas. Maybe some chocolate recipes..." Georgia trailed off.

"The price of roses is always a good topic," Alicia chimed in. "Maybe we could show them being grown and harvested, shipped to florists and delivered in a bouquet." Alicia, too, stopped talking and waited for his reaction.

For once, Tony wished for one of her outrageous ideas. "They'll do all that on the local news," he pointed out. From the women's expressions, he figured they were aware that the idea was weak.

Georgia slumped. "Oh, he's right."

"So what?" Alicia exclaimed. "This year, we just won't do the marriage proposals. If we explain why, people will understand."

Understanding didn't translate into market share. Tony wished he could send Georgia out of the room and have a heart-to-heart with Alicia. She was painting too bright a picture for her partner.

"Your Valentine special is your most popular show. Each year, you've increased your markets because of it. This year is no different. In fact, once we get the viewing numbers, I think it'll be time to go to the networks with 'Hartson Flowers'."

"Of course that's always been our goal," Alicia said, "but it'll have to wait until next year."

Tony could feel Georgia's eyes on him. He didn't dare look at her as he spoke candidly to Alicia. "You two have a great show and it's gaining in popularity. If you don't make your move this year, one of the networks will pilot their own version. When that happens, I won't be able to give your show away. We should move on this the day after your special airs."

"Oh, no!" Georgia wailed. "I've ruined everything!"

Alicia's eyes shot daggers at him. "Stop blaming yourself," she cooed to Georgia, her voice contrasting with her facial expression.

"I'm only pointing out that it would be in everyone's best interests to produce the Valentine special as scheduled. It can still be done, but Alicia will need help." Tony spoke heavily. Usually he didn't mind being the anchor for people whose heads were in the clouds. It was his lot in life to be one of the practical ones—a person to ground the dreamers. But he'd thought Alicia would have grasped the situation without him pointing it out to her. Instead, she insisted on being Miss Merry Sunshine for Georgia's benefit:

"I couldn't break somebody new in at this late date," she said. "We're scheduled to start filming on Monday."

How had a day that had begun so promisingly turned so sour? "You won't have to break in anybody new and you can proceed as scheduled,'' Tony told her. "I'll be your co-producer.''

Alicia was stunned. Anthony Domenico, the taciturn owner of Domenico Cable Productions, was offering to substitute for Georgia *himself*? "You can't be gone from the studio for three weeks!''

"Not easily, but I'll manage.''

"I—that isn't necessary. If taping the special is that important, someone else—''

Tony shook his head. "You said it yourself. You can't break in somebody new on a show this important.'' He stood, a tall man with dark hair and dark eyes, eyes that were always serious. Eyes that revealed nothing of himself or what he was thinking.

"I'd rather break in somebody new than fight with somebody old.''

"What's to fight about?'' he asked her. "The budget and programs are all set.''

Georgia murmured her agreement.

"I guarantee we'll find something,'' Alicia muttered. Of this, she was certain. Honestly, the more success she and Georgia achieved, the more conservative Tony became.

During the early years, she and Georgia had struggled before they found their voice and style. Tony supported them, even though some of those early attempts were less than successful.

Remembering, Alicia cringed. Truly, some were awful. Filled with her amateurish babbling and Georgia's constant posing like the beauty-pageant winner she was, it was amazing that "Hartson

Flowers'' survived. They had Tony to thank for that and Alicia was grateful to him, even though they'd fought on every story idea since then.

She understood his concern. Their show was his cash cow, his big money-maker. He'd never hidden that fact from them, another reason he had their loyalty.

But working for him was one thing—working *with* him was another. They barely spoke to each other now, as it was.

He didn't have the type of personality that appealed to her. His conversations were all business with no small talk or idle chitchat. If he didn't have anything to say, then he remained silent, though he scrupulously kept them informed of sales or feedback from his marketing efforts.

He never got excited about any of her ideas—simply wanted to know the details and the projected cost. Every time Georgia approached him, she'd return from their meeting with a watered-down version of Alicia's proposal. It got so Alicia was purposely outrageous just to get approval for what she wanted in the first place.

Working with him would be impossible. Just being in his office sapped her creative energy.

She'd been in here before, though not often. It was a plain office that said nothing about Tony except that he didn't have a big ego. For heaven's sake, their office was bigger than his. When he'd offered the space to them, she'd mentioned that fact. He'd responded that she and Georgia needed a large office and he didn't.

Even his wall calendar was plain white with big squares and no picture. His coffee mug was a solid black, devoid of company logos. There were no knickknacks on his file cabinets, no plants, no photographs, no interesting paperweights. It could have been anyone's office. Even the screen saver on his computer simply blacked out the screen.

She studied Tony as he questioned Georgia about her upcoming leave. He was a good-looking man— tall, dark and handsome due to his Italian ancestry—but intensely private. In the four years she'd worked for him, Alicia couldn't remember seeing him smile and had never heard about anyone who dated him. When they spoke, he'd never let one scrap of personal information slip out.

When she'd first affiliated with his studio, Alicia had been intrigued by him—that handsome face was hard to ignore—but had long ago given up ever getting to know him. Now she didn't want to.

And as important as the Valentine special was, she didn't think she could spend three weeks working so closely with him. She and Georgia bounced ideas off each other and were constantly tweaking the shows. She would never be able to re-create that kind of charged atmosphere with Tony Domenico.

He'd already walked around to his side of the desk, obviously searching for a notepad.

"Alicia, I'm going back to the office so you and Tony can discuss what you intend to do about the show." Georgia leveled a cautionary look at her.

Don't leave me, Alicia mouthed. She held out a hand to help Georgia lever herself out of the rolling chair.

Don't worry, Georgia mouthed back and squeezed her hand. *Everything will be fine.*

Alicia smiled weakly. She didn't want Georgia worrying, not that Georgia looked at all concerned.

"Okay, so where are we with this thing?" As he spoke, Tony sat in the chair Georgia had recently vacated.

Alicia was momentarily distracted by the fact that he was sitting right there next to her instead of behind his desk. Their knees were separated by mere inches and she was conscious that she'd never been this close to him before.

Conscious, too, of the crisp white shirt, opened at the throat, and the dark pants, meticulously creased. His fathomless black eyes gazed at her, waiting for her to answer, giving no clue to his own thoughts, though Georgia's announcement had to have thrown him off balance.

"Look, Tony...this won't work," she began. "We'd kill each other in three days."

"You're being overly optimistic again."

Alicia blinked. "Oh, my gosh, you've got a sense of humor." Who'd have thought it?

"And a sense of self-preservation. We need to produce this show for as much your sake as mine."

"Not 'we'." Slowly, she shook her head. "You don't even like 'Hartson Flowers'."

"I don't have to like it," he pointed out. "It's not my job to like it. I assure you that my likes and dislikes will have no bearing on my effectiveness as your production assistant."

"Well, it bothers *me* that you don't like it."

"Alicia." He sat back. "I admire you and Georgia and what you've done. I appreciate good work when I see it. You two have put together a compelling and audience-pleasing half hour that is growing in popularity. The businessman in me likes what you've accomplished. Personally . . ." He gestured with his hand, drawing Alicia's attention. She'd never noticed how smooth and well shaped his hands were before. "I don't have any use for romantic nonsense. But my personal tastes aren't going to get in the way of my doing a good job for you. I've had field experience, so you don't have to worry on that front."

During his entire speech, he hadn't altered his expression. He hadn't smiled. He'd pronounced. Dictated. Decreed. Just like her stepfather.

"We can't work together," she said. "We're already arguing. We always argue."

"We're not arguing, we're discussing."

Alicia threw up her hands and leaned back in her seat. The only reason she hadn't stormed out was because she knew she'd have to get used to working without Georgia. Might as well start now. She tried again. "Part of what makes our show so successful is the informal kidding around Georgia and I do, both on and off camera."

"You would be the only one appearing on camera," Tony said. "I should have made that clear. Sorry." He made a note.

Okay, she was going to have to be blunt. "You intimidate people. They feel uncomfortable around you."

The dark eyes didn't blink. "People in general, or just you?"

"*I'm* not intimidated by you, but we'll be working with people who are about to propose marriage. It's a huge step under ordinary circumstances, but try to imagine proposing in front of a camera crew. The people who contact us want something very romantic. They also want a sympathetic ear. You'll have to be prepared for that. You'd be surprised at the things they tell you. They need reassuring, too. Most of the people are men, but this year, we do have a woman who'll be proposing to her boyfriend. I'm just afraid—''

He interrupted her. ''Please give me some credit. I'm going along as behind-the-scenes support, so I'll avoid contaminating the happy couples with my presence.''

For the briefest moment, there was a flash of something in the depths of his eyes. Hurt? Alicia felt her cheeks warm.

''We're professionals,'' he continued. ''We can make this work.''

After that, what could she say? Argue that they *weren't* professionals? ''All right, then.'' She stood and held out her hand.

He grasped it with a surprisingly warm grip. ''I thought we were going to discuss details.''

''I'll get Georgia's notes and type something up for you.'' He was still holding her hand. She tugged and he released it immediately.

''I'll be waiting.'' He nodded to her and wheeled his chair back around his desk.

That was it?

Even though he wasn't a demonstrative man, Alicia had expected a little more gratitude. With a shrug, she headed for the door. Working with him was going to be frustrating, she'd known that.

When she reached the doorway, she turned. Tony was already occupied with something else. Impulsively, she called to him, "Do you think you could smile? Just once?"

"Why?" He didn't even look up.

"Because the Valentine special will be produced. Disaster is averted. You should be feeling happy. Victory is yours."

"You act like I won a battle." Putting down his pencil, he stared at her a moment. "You made the logical decision if you plan to approach the networks. I *am* pleased, though."

"So would it kill you to smile?"

She could see him consider her words.

"Is it important to you that I do so?"

She was *not* going to get along with this man at all. Why had she agreed to work with him? "Yes. Yes, it is." And the sooner he realized it, the better. Resolutely, she marched back over to his desk and planted her fists on the cluttered surface. "I'd like you to smile, just so I know you're capable of it."

His face could have been carved of Italian marble like the statues of his ancestors. When the seconds ticked by and he didn't move, Alicia knew she'd overstepped her bounds.

She was in the wrong. They were business associates of a different sort than her friendly relationship with Georgia. She had no right to criticize Tony Domenico's personal traits. "I'm sorry, I was out of line."

"Yes." His voice was very low.

"Well." Wasn't this humiliating? She stared at her toes. "I'll get that information to you." Turning on her heel, she retreated.

"Alicia?"

She glanced back.

"Thanks." For a moment, his dark eyes held hers.

And then he smiled.

Alicia remained rooted to the doorway. That smile transformed Tony Domenico from a robot into a human being. A man.

A very, very attractive man.

CHAPTER TWO

ALICIA blinked before backing through the doorway.

She hadn't even said, "You're welcome." She most certainly hadn't smiled back.

Get a grip. His smile was probably fake. Working in television, Alicia had seen her share of fake smiles. So what if Tony's was the best fake she'd ever seen? It was still fake and they were still stuck with each other for three weeks. She thought about the prospect all the way back to the office she shared with Georgia.

Actually, they had two offices, but found they were spending so much time running back and forth between the two, they'd moved their desks and phones into one and turned the other into an interview lounge.

It was like stepping into a different world. Pale peach walls and terra-cotta carpeting neutralized the greenish glare of fluorescent lighting. Buff-colored furniture and bleached wood paneling kept the atmosphere businesslike, yet feminine. Mint green pillows and office chairs added another touch of color. Of course, this decor clashed with the colors of every major holiday except Easter, but they worked around it.

"Hey, call the custodian to help you with those." Alicia quickened her pace when she discovered that Georgia was lifting boxes and files.

"I feel fine." Georgia dropped an armload of files into a cardboard box and propped her hands at her nonexistent waist. "In fact, I think I'm going to have a chat with my doctor. If I agree to cut back and work part-time, there's no reason for me to spend the next three months in bed."

"Don't be ridiculous. He said bed, you're going to bed." Alicia tilted her head so she could read the labels on the file folders. "You aren't taking anything I'll need, are you?"

"No. I thought I'd catch up on correspondence and contact some of these people who've suggested story ideas." Georgia turned troubled eyes toward Alicia. "Listen, I could go on location with you and rest just as easily in a hotel room as I can in my own home."

"And the point of that would be ... ?"

"To help you with the Valentine show."

"It appears that I already have help."

Georgia groaned. "I never dreamed Tony'd insist on taking my place." She bit her lip. "Do you hate me?"

Alicia hugged her. "No."

"But you hate Tony."

"I don't *hate* him." Alicia grimaced. "We just don't get along, that's all."

"And I have never been able to figure out why." Georgia scooped her entire In basket from her desk and set it in the box. "If you talk calmly to the man, he's actually quite reasonable."

"But he's so ..." Alicia clenched her hands. "*Bossy!*"

Georgia broke into laughter. "That's because he is a boss!"

"You know what I mean." Alicia crossed her arms and leaned against Georgia's desk. "He rejects all my ideas."

"He does not."

"Well, he hates them. He's always criticizing." She lowered her voice in imitation of Tony's baritone. "Do we need all these extras? Can't we cut some of this? Isn't there a cheaper way to get the same effect?" Her voice returned to normal. "I've heard that last one about a million times."

"That's his job. He's got to watch the budget."

"But just once, I'd like to hear him say, 'That's a great idea. Go with it.'"

"Tony doesn't sweat the small stuff. It's only your grandiose schemes that he questions." Georgia pointed to the wall by Alicia. "Would you roll up my calendar for me?"

"Gladly." Georgia's giant pink-and-red heart-shaped calendar was a decorating eyesore. Alicia unhooked it at once. "I don't see why we can't do a local Valentine special this year. It would be cheaper. That should make him happy."

"You heard Tony. He's already sold the show to as many markets as we had last year." Georgia accepted the rolled-up calendar. "People love watching the surprise proposals."

"I know." Alicia sighed. "They're so romantic." She smiled a dreamy smile. "The people are so much in love and want to share their happiness with the entire world. Don't you remember how you felt?"

"Drew proposed to me because the interest rates were low and it was a good time to buy a house."

Georgia put a rubber band around the calendar and dropped it into the box.

"You told me he put the proposal in a fortune cookie!"

Georgia rolled her eyes. "That made a better story. What really happened was that the fortune said, 'He who hesitates is lost' and Drew took that as a sign."

"I wish you hadn't told me." Alicia slumped on the edge of the desk. "All this time, I've been hoping to find someone as romantic as your husband. I want the diamond-ring-in-a-rose proposal. I want him to hire the orchestra at a supper club to play our song over and over while we dance alone on a smoke-filled floor."

"Do they even have supper clubs anymore?"

"They should." Alicia sighed again. "Or maybe he'll serenade me beneath a balcony."

Georgia waddled to the file cabinet and started sorting more files. "Your apartment is on the ground floor."

"Or while we're floating along the Grand Canal in Venice, with our gondolier singing Italian love songs."

"I've heard those canals really stink."

"Georgia! What's wrong with you? You're worse than Tony."

"My feet hurt and I can't take off my shoes because I won't be able to get them back on." She held out one foot. "Fat. Even my feet are fat."

"Then sit down, and I'll help you pull files."

Instead of arguing with her, Georgia lowered herself into a chair. She must be feeling the strain of her pregnancy, and Alicia was determined to send her home worry free.

Lifting out hanging folders for Georgia, she said, "Actually, I'm only letting off steam. The show will be wonderful, and Tony and I'll get along fine." *As long as we never see or speak to each other.* Alicia hoped Georgia was buying this. "I just don't want to do the show without you."

"I don't want you to do it without me, either."

Alicia felt a pang. She was going to miss Georgia. The nearly three months until the babies were born and then the three months they'd planned for Georgia to take care of her newborns meant working half a year without her partner. After the special, there would be weeks of shows to do before Georgia's return. Alicia wondered if Tony would insist on co-producing them with her, as well.

"I mean," Georgia continued with a shaky laugh, "what if you decide you like working with Tony better than working with me?"

Alicia felt Georgia's forehead with the back of her hand. "Hmm. No fever."

Georgia pushed her hand away. "No, really. He's experienced . . . handsome—"

"That man is like a storm cloud on a sunny day." Alicia closed the top file drawer and began sorting through the one underneath.

"He's just being professional."

"He's a professional grump. He's always talking unit costs and production time and numbers, numbers, numbers!" Alicia put her hand to her temple. "It gives me a headache."

"Faker." Georgia laughed. "*I* talk numbers with him and you know it!"

"Yes, but I listen outside the door."

Georgia blinked in surprise. "No way!"

Alicia grinned.

"Come on, I can't tell if you're kidding or not."

Alicia batted her eyes.

"You little sneak!" Georgia stared at her. "Oooh, I'm gonna get you for this! Now every time I go into his office, I'll wonder if you're eavesdropping."

"Well, you won't have to go into his office for months, so you can forget about it," Alicia said.

With a haughty look on her face, Georgia reached across the desk top for her Rolodex and pencil holder and dropped them into the box. "I think from now on, you can negotiate with him yourself."

"Oh, no. Anything but that!" Alicia brought her hands together like a heroine in a melodrama. "Please, please don't make me."

"I think it would be good for you."

"No, it would be bad for me. He's like a giant creative sinkhole. A vacuum sucking out all my ideas." She drew air in between her teeth.

Georgia bubbled with laughter and Alicia joined her, glad her friend and partner had regained her good humor. How could Georgia think for one minute that Alicia would prefer working with Tony?

She scanned the second file drawer. "These are your local sources. You want any of them?"

"Better let me check."

Alicia lifted a stack and brought it over to Georgia.

"You know, I think part of your problem is the way you react to Tony." Georgia cleared a spot on her desk top for the files. "He's not your step-father and you're not your mother."

"Where did *that* come from?"

"The Mother's Day special we did year before last. I met your family, remember? And they also visited us here at the studio that time."

Alicia remembered all too well. "So?"

Georgia looked up from the file folders. "Your stepfather is very..." She trailed off with a delicate movement of her hand.

"He's a dictatorial, tyrannical skinflint." And that was being kind.

"Dictatorial and tyrannical are synonymous."

"Not with him." Alicia felt her stomach churn and began her deep-breathing exercises. Closing her eyes, she mentally transported herself to the beach where she could watch and listen to the waves lap at the shore. Breathe in—smell that sea air—breathe out—feel the sun warm her shoulders and relax the tense muscles. When she felt calmer, Alicia opened her eyes to find Georgia regarding her knowingly. "My relationship with my mother's husband has nothing to do with how I relate to Tony."

"I think it does. Your stepfather criticized every-thing from the number of suit jackets we keep in the closet to the cost of soft drinks from the vending machine and how many you consumed."

Alicia resumed her hunt in the file cabinet. "I didn't realize you were paying that much attention."

"I couldn't help it. You turned from my partner into a little girl. You ran around justifying *every-thing* to that man. It was *incredible*."

Alicia wished the twins would kick Georgia or something.

"And your mother constantly hushed you. She sounded like a leaking balloon."

"She doesn't want to *upset* him," Alicia mumbled. "She never wanted to *upset* him. He might throw her out and then what would she do? It was bad enough that he was supporting another man's child. I should be grateful to have a roof over my head." Alicia stopped abruptly. As close as she and Georgia had become, she'd never discussed her family with her partner. And she didn't want to now. She tried visualizing the beach again.

"You've resented your mother because she wouldn't stand up to your stepfather. So, you re-create the situation with Tony, only he plays the part of your stepfather and you play your mother. Very common."

"That's ridiculous. I knew I shouldn't have let you interview that new pop psychologist."

"She's a highly respected family therapist." Georgia softened her voice. "But I didn't mean to upset you. Just give Tony a chance, okay?" She smiled. "Who knows? He might turn out to be the man of your dreams. And don't make a crack about nightmares."

Clutching file folders to her chest, Alicia slowly turned around. "The man of my dreams is wildly, extravagantly romantic. It will be love at first sight and he won't be disguised as Tony Domenico."

At seven o'clock, Tony stretched his arms high above his head and decided to call it a night. He didn't look forward to spending three weeks away from his office and sincerely hoped Alicia had incorporated editing time into that estimate. Maybe he'd only be gone a couple of weeks. Maybe ten days, if they were lucky and efficient—as if it were possible for romance and efficiency to co-exist.

He'd spent the rest of the afternoon delegating as much as he could and trying to catch up on what he couldn't, but still planned to devote Saturday and Sunday to preparing for his absence.

"Oh, good. You're still here." Alicia breezed through the doorway without knocking.

Tony hadn't heard her approach. She offered him a tentative smile and he wondered whether or not she now expected him to grin like a fool every time they made eye contact.

Apparently not. "I've got Georgia's notes right here. It took longer than I thought to type them up." She thrust several pages at him and sighed, running her fingers through her short hair.

"Thanks." Tony scanned the sheets, looking for any holes in the preparation. Georgia had screened and selected the Valentine couples and even had three backups in case of any romantic or practical glitches. Not bad. "Do you need anything?" He flipped a page and studied the timetable Alicia had provided.

"I think we're all set."

"You've allocated the entire three weeks to filming. Editing on top of that?"

"Just studio tweaking after we get back."

Alicia sat on the edge of his desk and crossed her legs. Since she was wearing a short skirt, Tony could see several inches above her knees. She had good television legs. Tony had never bothered to look at them in person before, but he'd never been close to eye level with them before, either.

She leaned forward to point at something on the page and he caught the faint suggestion of the perfume she must have applied that morning. "I allowed three days on location for each taping—plus one extra for the first one. There are animals involved."

Tony winced. "Not animals."

"Animals," Alicia said firmly. "A circus parade, to be exact."

He'd been hoping that meant only clowns. "A circus parade? For a marriage proposal? What gets into people?"

Alicia got a determined look on her face. "I think it's romantic." Her tone dared him to argue.

"It sounds like a lot of trouble." It could be worse, Tony thought to himself. It could be babies. Babies were the only thing worse than animals. At least animals could be trained and could work longer hours than human babies.

"The visuals will be worth it. And—" Alicia tapped the middle proposal's shooting schedule "—this one might take an extra day, as well. I don't know. It depends on the weather. I allowed for a Friday return to give the crew a weekend off, so actually, we're talking about nineteen days. Three of those are time off and two are cushion. The rest is travel time."

"When do you plan to edit?"

Alicia hopped off the desk. "I edit as I go and I can come in that weekend after we get back for the studio work, if you think I need to. I'll also be sending raw footage to Georgia. She'll write narration for us."

"Sounds good." It did. Tony relaxed somewhat. They'd actually had a conversation without Alicia's exploding.

"Okay, then I'm off and I'll see you bright and early Monday morning." Waggling her fingers, she slipped from the room as suddenly as she'd entered it.

Tony gazed after her. Why couldn't all their encounters be so easy? He'd never liked watching his every word around her. He couldn't ask for clarification, make a comment or suggestion without Alicia erupting. He'd heard Georgia ask questions or raise objections and Alicia didn't snap at her. Why was he so different? He wasn't an unreasonable man, simply a cautious one.

Shrugging off the question, he put Alicia's schedule into a file folder. He'd study it tomorrow morning. In the meantime, it was Friday night, which meant a visit to his parents. His day just kept getting better and better.

The elder Domenicos lived in an older section of Houston filled with fifties-style bungalows and huge trees. Tony and his elder sister had grown up in the small house and his sister lived there still—with her unemployed poet husband and three children.

Tony had to bite his tongue during every visit.

He was later than usual tonight and supposed they'd already eaten. They hadn't.

"Tony!" His mother threw open the door as soon as his steps caused the wooden porch to squeak. Enveloping him in a tomato-and-basil-scented hug, she led him into the house.

The first thing Tony saw was a huge bouquet of roses—more than a dozen. The arrangement had to have cost at least a hundred dollars.

"You see my roses?" His mother, Vivian, asked, obviously delighted.

"Yes." They were hard to miss as was the loving smile his father wore while he watched his wife fuss over the flowers.

"Have some wine, Tony." Without waiting for a response, Robert Domenico splashed some red wine into a goblet and shoved it across the kitchen table toward him.

"What are we celebrating?" Tony asked, an oblique reference to the expensive label on the wine.

"Life," his father answered with an expansive gesture. "You don't have to have a reason to celebrate."

Tony's eyes slid to the roses as he sipped the wine. If his father had to celebrate, why didn't he celebrate with a new screen for the front door? Or recover the den couch Tony's mother had bemoaned?

"Your father is such a romantic," Vivian said, as if Tony didn't already know. Standing behind her husband as he sat at the table, she leaned down and hugged him before returning to stir a pot of sauce simmering on the stove.

"The roses make her happy," his father told him. "And when she's happy, I'm happy."

His parents exchanged fond smiles, as though being happy was the most important thing in the world. And to them, Tony knew it was.

"Peter? Is that—oh, hi, Tony." His sister, Thea, carried a baby into the kitchen. "I thought I heard Peter come in." She looked around for her husband. "He's at a poetry reading," she announced, pride evident. "He was invited to read *two* of his poems."

"That's great." Especially if he managed to sell any of his poetry. Tony knew better than to ask.

"Uncle Tony!" shrieked two pajama-clad girls and flung themselves at his leg.

"Hey—watch it. I'll spill..." Miraculously, the sloshing red wine remained in the goblet. He set it on the table and hugged his nieces. They giggled, then raced back to the bedroom.

"It's my turn to sit in the beanbag chair," yelled the younger one.

"They're watching a tape," Thea explained. "I don't know how I lived without a video recorder." She smiled at him. "Thanks."

"Has Peter unbent enough to watch a tape?" Tony's brother-in-law barely tolerated television. He hadn't been happy when Tony had given the family a VCR last Christmas. But Tony knew how Thea struggled to keep the children quiet when her husband wanted to write and he'd thought this would help.

"Yes, but don't let him know I told you."

As they shared a smile, Tony's nephew reached for his tie and tried to put it into his mouth. "Hey there, sport, silk and drool don't mix." Tony gently pried the baby's fingers off. "Speaking of clothes, what are those fancy pants you're wearing?"

"Tea towels, Uncle Tony." Thea spoke in a baby voice and nuzzled her son's stomach, making him laugh.

"Thea?"

"I ran out of diapers and Peter had to borrow Papa's car. Ours is in the shop."

"Again?"

She wrinkled her nose. "Still."

"What's wrong with it?"

"Nothing," she replied breezily. "When Peter has the money to pay the repair bill, we'll get it back."

"You should have said something. I—"

"Don't worry about it, Tony. Paulie doesn't know the difference. Does he?" Thea tickled her son and he gurgled again. Grinning, she whisked him out of the room.

"You worry too much," his father said. "Peter is using my car until his is ready."

"And what are you using?" Tony asked.

"My legs." His father laughed. "Today, I walked and because I walked, I saw these roses." He gestured to the huge bouquet. "And next to the florist, I found a man who sells wine. Good wine. And next to his shop was a baker. If I'd been driving my car, I would have missed these things." His father beamed. "Sometimes, we need to slow down to live life. You should try walking sometimes, Tony."

"He should try eating, Robert." Vivian shook salt into the water boiling on the stove. "He's too thin."

Tony forced a smile.

When his father looked at the roses, he saw love. Tony saw the expense. A car sat in the shop because they couldn't afford the repair bill, his nephew had run out of diapers, but two dozen roses sat in his mother's kitchen.

Tony's family had the ability to soar with life and not worry about bumpy landings. Tony couldn't even get off the ground. He spent his life watching and envying them—and building safety nets for the inevitable crashes.

He'd brought one of his safety nets with him this evening. Retrieving his wine, he raised the glass. "Perhaps there is a reason to celebrate."

His mother clasped her hands together. "You've met a girl!"

In spite of himself, Tony thought of Alicia. "No, Ma." Though Alicia would fit right in with his impractical family. "I brought your quarterly dividend." Reaching into his breast pocket, Tony withdrew an envelope and handed it to his father. "It's a little bigger than usual."

"You see, Tony?" His father tapped the envelope. "All this worrying about us isn't necessary."

"Only because our Tony is so clever. I told you investing in our son was better than putting our money in somebody's fund." Vivian bustled over and hugged him.

Robert shook his head. "He's clever, but he still works too hard."

"Speaking of work," Tony said to change the subject, "I'll be going out of town on Monday."

"Will you be gone long?" his mother asked on her way back to the kitchen.

"A couple of weeks. Maybe three. One of my producers has to go on early maternity leave. She's having twins."

"Ah." His mother smiled, her features softening. "Two babies. How wonderful."

Why did everyone think twins were wonderful? Having baby-sat his nieces and nephew on occasion, Tony felt one baby at a time was more than enough.

"I live for the day when you come to me and tell me you're giving me grandchildren," Vivian said.

"You already have grandchildren," Tony pointed out. Uselessly, he knew. He was the only son. His children would bear the Domenico name. Tony wasn't opposed to having children. They simply weren't high on his list of priorities.

The front door banged. "Greetings all!" a theatrical voice rang out. Peter had returned. "I've had a stunning success and we must celebrate accordingly!"

"What, what?"

Tony could hear Thea's excited voice. Seconds later, Peter, a bearded, long-haired man, appeared in the kitchen doorway bearing a bottle of champagne.

"That's the real thing," Tony said after glancing at the label. Peter must have finally sold something.

The girls swooped down on their father and Tony's parents beamed as their son-in-law recounted his great success. "And they want me to submit twenty of my best poems to them," he concluded.

"So they're going to publish your poems?" Tony asked, after congratulating Peter.

"It's not certain yet," Peter began.

"But they surely will when they read his poems," Thea declared, and looked adoringly up at her husband.

"It's a literary anthology," Peter explained. "Highly regarded. Quite an honor simply to be considered."

Literary, meaning little or no money involved. Tony had no problem with Peter's writing poetry, but he had a very big problem with the fact that Peter had no regular gainful employment to support his family while he waited for success.

While Thea helped her mother with last-minute dinner preparations, Peter drew Tony aside. "The money's not there yet, but when it is, I'm going to let you handle it. I saw that last dividend check."

"I'm not in the financial planning business," Tony demurred.

"You obviously know something." Peter laughed, his rich voice filling the room. He clapped Tony across the shoulders. "And I want to invest in your company, too. Pop Domenico has sure done all right."

Tony chose his next words carefully. His father's modest "investment" had simply been a vehicle for Tony to give his parents money without their knowing he was doing so. If they kept abreast of financial markets at all, they would realize that recouping more than the original investment every year was unusual.

"That was a once in a lifetime deal," he said, but Robert Domenico had opened the champagne and was proposing a toast. After that, Peter proceeded to recite one of his poems.

His daughters sat in his lap with Thea looking on adoringly. Even the baby was quiet. Tony's parents were holding hands.

Though he wanted to, Tony didn't understand the appeal of the poem and was conscious that he was the only one in the room who didn't.

Alicia Hartson would have. This was just the sort of sappy stuff she liked. He had no doubt that she would have been thrilled for his brother-in-law. Tony imagined her enjoying the champagne without thinking of the cost. He could see her blond head as she buried her nose in the roses. She'd probably think diapering a baby in tea towels was cute.

Alicia Hartson was, in fact, exactly like his impractical family. He didn't have to work with them, but he was going to have to work with her.

He shuddered. How was he going to endure the next three weeks?

CHAPTER THREE

"I'LL DRIVE," Tony announced. He held out his hand for the car keys.

Alicia considered protesting, but after one look at Tony's fathomless eyes and the impatient set to his mouth, she silently dropped the keys into his open palm. It wouldn't do to begin their work together with an argument.

She always drove when she and Georgia went on location. Georgia liked to review the setup and make incessant telephone calls from the car. Georgia could probably rule the world by telephone.

But she wasn't with Georgia; she was with a dark-eyed grump.

Walking around to the passenger side, Alicia carefully set her briefcase and laptop computer on the seat beside Tony, decided it looked too much as though she wanted to avoid any contact with him and moved them to the back with the small snack cooler she'd stored there earlier.

Tony checked his watch and gazed straight ahead without saying anything. His ringless hands gripped the steering wheel. A finger tapped in time to the passing seconds.

So they were a few minutes behind schedule. So it wasn't the crack of dawn. Now was not the time to be a stickler about schedules. "We're still fine," Alicia felt compelled to tell him. "There's slack in my schedule for just this reason."

"Each minute we delay starting will add at least ten minutes sitting on the highway in the morning rush hour," Tony stated.

Alicia was drawing on her reserve of patience already. Not a good sign. "One of the battery cells for the Minicam went out. No one could have predicted it. The crew caught it this morning during the final equipment check. Wasn't it fortunate that we didn't get all the way to Brownsville and *then* discover we needed a new battery?"

Slowly, he turned his head. "Why wasn't the equipment checked last night?"

Alicia matched his clipped tone. "Why wasn't your studio equipment working?"

"No one but your crew has ever used that camera," Tony replied. "I can't repair what I don't know is broken. I repeat, why wasn't the equipment checked last night?"

She resented his question and she resented the superior tone in which he asked it. "Last night was Sunday, which would have incurred overtime charges. I feel money is better spent in front of the camera rather than behind it."

"If you don't have a working camera, it's a moot point."

Alicia did not appreciate his criticism. As she'd told him, she built in time to absorb glitches like this. And this was a very minor glitch. If Tony got so bent out of shape over a small equipment failure, then he wouldn't be able to tolerate the unexpected problems they were certain to encounter. Rather than point out that she and Georgia had successfully produced their show for four years without his input, Alicia asked, "Did you eat breakfast this morning?"

He was silent for so long, Alicia wasn't certain he'd answer. "I had a cup of coffee."

"That explains why you're so grouchy. You know better than to skip breakfast." Getting on her knees, she turned and lifted the lid of her cooler. "Here." She handed him a box with a straw. "Drink this."

"I'm not thirsty."

"It's pineapple orange juice. You need something in your stomach."

"I don't—"

Alicia let go of the cold box knowing Tony would automatically catch it. He did. She withdrew a plastic bag from within the cooler and sat back down. "Eat one of these with your juice. They're energy bars. I made them myself." She dug in the bag and held out a brown square. "They've got oat bran, wheat germ, rice germ and whole wheat flour with ground nuts, dried cranberries and blueberries because I hate raisins. You aren't allergic to any of that are you?"

"Not that I—"

"Then eat this." She grabbed the hand that wasn't holding the juice box and put the brown square in it. "I'm not going to be driven by somebody who hasn't properly fueled his body. Tests show that skipping breakfast leads to—"

"If I eat this, will you be quiet?" Tony interrupted.

"If you eat that, I won't lecture you on skipping breakfast anymore."

His gaze flicked from her to the lump in his hand then back to her again. "Deal." He popped the

square into his mouth, chewing while he opened
the juice box. "My nieces drink these." He worked
the straw into the hole.

My nieces drink these. The man had nieces, which
meant he had either a brother or a sister or both
or several. He had a family.

Alicia had never thought of Tony Domenico with
a family. His office contained no pictures or juvenile drawings stuck to the bulletin board. He never
discussed his personal life and neither she nor
Georgia had ever asked. Tony hadn't seemed like
the sort of man who'd answer personal questions
and his conversations hadn't lent themselves to idle
chitchat. She wanted to ask about his nieces now,
but was afraid to pounce on the first piece of personal information he'd ever let drop. He was
probably just thinking aloud anyway.

She watched as he finished the juice in one con-
tinuous draw, his cheekbones defined by his pursed
mouth.

"I'm going to throw this away," he said when
he finished. "No sense in starting a long trip with
trash in the car."

He climbed out, a long-legged man in jeans and
a knit shirt. He looked as good in casual clothes
as he did in more formal office attire. Alicia ducked
her head so she could watch his progress across the
parking lot toward the trash receptacle by the studio's back door. Tony moved with an unstudied,
unselfconscious stride, confident, yet swagger free.

Slowly, Alicia relaxed into the car seat and faced
straight ahead. She'd worked at Domenico Cable
Productions for nearly four years and had not
noticed Anthony Domenico as a man since the early

days, after it had become clear that they couldn't hold a civil conversation together.

So why was she noticing him now? What had changed? A few brief moments of civility?

No, it was his smile. She'd seen him smile and where there was a smile, there was hope. Now that she knew he was capable of smiling, she wanted to see him smile again. Of course, if her crew didn't hurry up, she probably never would.

She closed the plastic bag containing her energy bars and returned it to the cooler. Tony was walking back to the car. Alicia deliberately avoided looking at him.

"They're ready," he announced, slammed the door and started the car before Alicia had a chance to fasten her seat belt. She did notice that he waited until she'd clicked it into place before driving out of the parking lot. He was impatient, not reckless.

The "Hartson Flowers" van, containing two camera crewmen and a sound technician, plus equipment, pulled out behind them. They began the drive south from Houston to Brownsville. Since they were traveling against the morning traffic, Alicia didn't think the road was very crowded. She didn't dare say anything about it, though. In fact, she didn't say anything at all. The hum of the engine and the faint road noise were the only sounds in the car. Tony didn't turn on the radio, either.

Alicia gazed at the flat landscape and thought about the hours ahead. She really missed Georgia.

After an hour, even her silence got on Tony's nerves. Alicia not talking was nearly as irritating as Alicia talking. He was aware of each re-

proachful glance she sent his way, each muffled sigh
as she gazed at the passing landscape.

Well, what had she expected when she forced him
to eat health food like that? Nuts and berries—he
should have known she was the nuts-and-berries
type.

In spite of their agreement, he hadn't expected
her to remain totally silent—hadn't thought her
capable of it.

She was fidgeting and trying not to show it.

"Why don't you fill me in on the three couples
you and Georgia have chosen?" Tony asked when
he couldn't stand it any longer. Though he didn't
look at her directly, he sensed her surprise at his
question, but she said nothing.

Reaching in the back for her briefcase, she flipped
it open. That was unexpected. He would have supposed she'd be able to recite the information off
the top of her head.

"Yesterday, I called Raul Garza in Brownsville
to reconfirm that he wanted to propose to Lillie
Patterson on camera for airing on 'Hartson
Flowers'." She held up a paper. "This is the release
he signed."

"I'm certain you have everything in order," Tony
said.

"I do."

He felt her gaze on him and shifted his eyes away
from the road long enough to contact hers. They
were blue. A cool, professionally detached blue.
One might say an icy blue. Or an irritated blue.

"I meant..." He wasn't used to explaining
himself. He also wasn't used to not being in charge
and reminded himself that this was her show and

he should defer to her. She'd taken his query as implied criticism when he hadn't intended any. "I wondered how you and Georgia find these people."

"*These people*," Alicia said with just the slightest emphasis, "write to us. We broadcast an invitation around Thanksgiving time for anyone who'd like to appear on our Valentine show to write to us and describe the way he or she plans to propose marriage."

"And a lot of people respond?"

"Yes, believe it or not, over a hundred sent letters and pictures and faxes. Most were men."

"Men?" Yeah, right. "And you don't think they were put up to it by their girlfriends?"

"We weed those out during our screening process. The appeal to our viewers is the surprise of the person who's receiving the proposal."

Tony had a difficult time believing that many men were aware of "Hartson Flowers". However, the tone in Alicia's voice warned him that she was still irritated with him. "It can't be too much of a surprise. A guy wouldn't risk being shot down on camera."

"Oh, but they do. Besides, Georgia has a sixth sense about relationships. In fact, after talking to some of the people, she'll just shake her head and say, 'That couple won't be kissing under the mistletoe.'"

"What?"

Tony heard her sigh faintly. "Meaning they'll break up by Christmas."

"I see."

"In the past, we've had couples drop out because they couldn't wait for us to tape them.

Christmas seems to be a popular time to give engagement rings."

Talking with Alicia wasn't so bad. When she restrained her bright, cheery, TV personality chatter, she was actually tolerable. But he could hear it bubbling beneath the surface just waiting to burst forth like the pressure behind a champagne cork. "Is that why you have so many backup couples?"

"I wish we had more," she admitted to Tony's consternation. "But it isn't fair to ask them to hold off on becoming engaged because they *might* be on our show."

"If Georgia does such a good screening job, why would you want more backup couples?" If Alicia wanted more, that meant there was a high failure rate with the primary couples. Failure was costly and time-consuming. Failure gave him headaches.

Alicia shifted around and returned her briefcase to the back seat. "We're dealing with *people* here, Tony. It's good television for us, but it's *their* lives. They don't care about our ratings or our time schedules. They aren't professionals and they're nervous. Have you ever proposed to a woman?"

The question caught him off guard. How had his life gotten into this discussion? She'd asked the question casually and he decided he'd answer it in the same spirit. "No."

She shrugged and tucked her legs under her. He'd noticed her legs yesterday. They looked just as fine today. He squinted at the road so her legs were no longer visible to him.

"I was going to ask if you'd been nervous...you've probably been nervous when you asked out a girl in high school. Imagine being a hundred times more nervous—and knowing there are cameras recording your every move." Shuddering, she continued, "I'm surprised we find *any* men willing to propose for our show."

"You said there were also women."

"Not many. It's still every little girl's fantasy that someday, Mr. Right will ask her to marry him and they'll live happily ever after."

Alicia's voice had changed, had grown softer. Tony wondered if she was aware of it. Her head was tilted to one side and she was staring out the windshield.

Was she remembering—or dreaming? Was there a Mr. Right in her life? Tony truly had no idea—he'd never cared one way or the other before. Her personal life was none of his business. And yet…he had to know. "Is that the way your proposal was?"

"Hmm?" Her head jerked toward him. "I didn't hear what you said."

Great. He shouldn't have asked the question in the first place. "I asked about your own proposal."

She blinked. "I haven't had one yet."

You had to ask. Now what should he say?

"But I know it will be the most romantic moment in my entire life," Alicia continued, saving Tony from an awkward reply. "And I know because that's the kind of man I'll fall in love with."

Implying that it would be impossible for her to love any other sort of man. Implying that a rose-bearing, poetry-spouting man was superior to any other kind of man.

Another woman like his mother and sister.

For reasons he didn't understand, Tony was disappointed in Alicia. She'd seemed a savvy enough type not to be taken in by men who used flowery talk to compensate for their other failings. Men who would then charm their women into forgetting that they couldn't hold a steady job or remember to come home each night.

Tony shook his head.

"Are you getting tired of driving?" Alicia asked. "Research shows that drivers should take a break every two hours when driving on long trips. I think that's a good idea for passengers, as well." She pointed to one of the many landscaped rest stops along the highway.

He could have driven the seven hours straight through to Brownsville with just a stop for refueling, but obligingly pulled into the rest stop. The van pulled in behind them.

Alicia jumped out of the car and began a series of stretching exercises. "Come on, Tony! Get out and get the blood flowing."

To his surprise, the "Hartson Flowers" crew in the van had piled out and were joining Alicia in her exercises. It was a crowded rest stop and people were staring. Of course, having the "Hartson Flowers" logo emblazoned on the side of the equipment van might have had something to do with it, too.

Alicia jogged around to the driver's side of the car and pulled open the door. "Get out of the car, Tony!" She jogged in place.

This time, he did. Giving in to Alicia Hartson was obviously the only way to keep her quiet.

"Do you want me to take a turn at driving now?" she asked at the end of their exercise session.

"No, I'm fine." He did feel more alert, he had to admit. "Stopping was a good idea."

Raising an eyebrow, she gazed at him across the car roof. "Why, Tony...was that a compliment?"

"I suppose so."

"Thank you," she chirped and got into the car.

Tony had a feeling that she'd been telling him something else. Why couldn't women come out and say what they meant? It would save everybody a lot of time.

The rest of the way to Brownsville, Tony was careful to keep the conversation strictly on business topics. He closely questioned Alicia about costs, scheduling and various what ifs, not caring whether she took offense or not. His production company was picking up the tab after all. She might be in charge of this program, but he had every right to know the inner workings of her show.

Alicia hadn't taken offense that he could tell. She answered each question smoothly and without hesitation, which told Tony that she'd anticipated many potential pitfalls and had already dealt with them. In spite of himself, Tony was impressed with how much work and how thorough a job she and Georgia had done.

He slid a glance toward Alicia's profile. Maybe it was actually possible they'd make it through without a major battle.

Alicia looked up from the map. "I think you want the next exit." She consulted the written directions she'd been given by Raul Garza. "Yes. This is it."

At last, after a drive that had seemed twelve times longer than it had been, they'd arrived in the southern Texas city of Brownsville. In a little while, she could escape the tension in the car.

The strained conversation had exhausted her. It wasn't Tony's fault. In fact, she suspected—no, she *knew*—that he felt exactly the same way. They couldn't relax around each other. He'd tried, and she gave him points for that. Idle conversation didn't come easy to him. Alicia knew he communicated when he had something to say and was silent when he didn't. Throwing out topics and seeing where they led wasn't his style, and yet, there he was, throwing with the best of them.

She appreciated his efforts, and had tried to help him out by talking at length until she realized he wished she'd be quiet and so she would be. After several miles of silence, he'd figure out she was being quiet on purpose and would ask her a question and the whole cycle would repeat.

Most of the time, their discussions ended when it became apparent that they held different views. Opposing views. Rather than argue, each stepped back. Alicia had not realized it was possible to find a person who disagreed with her on virtually everything.

Quite simply, she and her handsome boss were not sympatico. Unfortunate, but it didn't really matter. She was here to do a job and so was he.

"Before we go by Lillie Patterson's house, we'll send the crew to check us into the motel. We don't want to chance her seeing the van and spoiling the surprise," she said.

"Shall I stop at a service station so you can tell the crew?" Tony asked.

Alicia had already lowered the window. "Oh, no. They know the drill." She waved at the van and rolled the window back up.

"But how do you know where they're going?"

Don't lose your temper. You've made it this far. "We have reservations here." *Which I put in your report.* "And, of course, there is the cell phone." She patted her purse.

He made a small sound. "I keep forgetting about those. I don't have one."

"Why not?"

Tony hesitated. "I suppose because I'm either at my home or in my office, or on the way between the two."

What a drab life he led. Maybe that was the reason he never discussed his personal life—he didn't have one. "We're looking for Oakwood Drive," she said. "You'll need to turn right."

Tony's mouth tightened and he pulled off the street into a fast-food-restaurant parking lot. "May I see the map?"

"I have instructions." Men had this macho thing about following directions.

"We passed Oakwood two streets back."

While she was going on about cellular telephones and mentally chastising him. Silently, Alicia surrendered her map.

When they finally turned onto Lillie Patterson's street, Alicia swallowed a groan. It was a narrow two-lane street with several cars parked in front of the houses.

"And I was wondering how you were going to *find* a circus. Now I'm wondering what you're going to do when you get one," Tony said. Lurking under his dry tone was the faintest hint of amusement.

Alicia might have been intrigued if his amusement hadn't been at her expense. "The Ramon Family Circus winters here in Brownsville. I wouldn't come here without verifying something so basic."

Tony gestured to the street. "Mr. Garza wants to parade this circus past his girlfriend's house?"

"Yes."

"I think it's time we had a chat with him and see if he's thought this thing through."

Alicia handed the directions to Raul Garza's house to Tony, then tried to figure out the logistics of parading elephants and so forth down the narrow residential street. If Georgia were here, they'd brainstorm. Tony had already decided it was impossible. She could tell just by looking at his face.

Drat. Grabbing her cell phone, Alicia punched in Georgia's number, not caring that Tony would overhear her conversation.

"Georgia!" At the sound of her friend and partner's voice, Alicia's tense muscles eased. She chatted with Georgia for a few moments until she became aware of Tony's impatient glances as he maneuvered the car through the city. "Listen, we're on location for Garza-Patterson. We haven't talked with Raul yet, but let me tell you there isn't much room. The only circus fitting down this street will be a flea circus."

Alicia could hear tapping and knew Georgia was accessing the Garza file on her laptop.

"Sugar, I talked to him about that. He assured me there was plenty of room."

"I don't know...the front yards are small, too, with several cars parked along the curb. That's going to be a problem."

"I don't see that there's a problem," Tony broke in. "We'll talk to the guy and tell him it won't work. Then we'll go on to couple number two."

Alicia sent him a withering glance.

"I heard that," Georgia said. "Are you letting him bully you, Alicia?"

"Not yet," she replied. "I do want to talk with Raul and then I'll get back with you. Be thinking."

"Gotcha."

Alicia broke the connection with Georgia and immediately punched in Raul's number. In spite of the late start in leaving Houston, they were forty-five minutes ahead of schedule. Georgia drove fast, which was one reason Alicia didn't let her drive very often. Tony must have driven like lightning. On the other hand, she, Tony and the crew hadn't lingered over lunch the way she and Georgia did, so maybe Tony hadn't driven all that fast. The trip certainly hadn't seemed fast.

She was going to have to stop comparing Tony to Georgia. At least he was here with her. It couldn't have been easy for him to rearrange his schedule on such short notice and all she'd done was gripe to herself about the situation. Not very mature. Alicia resolved to make more of an effort to be pleasant and tolerant of Tony's more restrained personality.

Even if she had to bite her tongue to do so.

Raul Garza was expecting them. "I can't believe you're really here!" He grinned and ushered them into his small apartment.

"One of us is anyway," Alicia said. "This is Anthony Domenico, who markets 'Hartson Flowers'. He's assisting me because Georgia has been confined to bed for the rest of her pregnancy."

"She's all right?" The young man's face creased with concern.

"Oh, yes. She's having twins."

"Twins! That's great!" He beamed at Alicia. When he met Tony's gaze, Alicia noticed that Raul's smile faded.

"Don't mind him. He's thinking of all the work that'll be waiting for him when he gets back." Couldn't the man at least try to act pleasant? Alicia took Raul's arm and led him to the leather sofa. "We've been by Lillie's house," she began as she took out her notebook, "and we need to discuss the logistics."

Tony could hardly stand to remain silent. This whole circus bit was getting way out of hand. At least Raul had a circus. According to him, the Ramon Family Circus toured the Southwest and spent winters in Brownsville, where the weather would stay mild throughout the off season. Apparently, Raul and Lillie had met while trying out for the circus when they were youngsters.

"We wanted to run away with the circus, you know? We saw the kids and thought, hey, they don't have to go to school and they can eat all the cotton candy and popcorn they want. They can see the shows for free, you know?"

Alicia was nodding, smiling and scribbling notes. Why, Tony couldn't guess. What happened to discussing logistics?

"What did you want to do with the circus?" she asked. "I realize you discussed this with Georgia, but Tony and I'd like to hear your story again."

Actually, Tony didn't particularly care about Raul Garza's childhood dreams. Why didn't Alicia tell the man that a circus parade down his girlfriend's street was impossible? Why were they wasting time?

"I wanted to be the guy who rode the motorcycle on that spinning ball, you know? Lillie, she just wanted to wear pretty costumes and ride elephants."

"Elephants." Alicia nodded and made a note.

"We practiced. Lots."

"How did she practice riding an elephant?" Tony asked and heard Alicia stifle an irritated sigh.

"Uh, she had a really fat horse." Raul laughed.

Tony didn't. He could read Alicia's mind as clearly as if she'd spoken. She was going to try to get that woman on an elephant. He'd bet on it.

"And she made costumes?" Alicia asked.

"For me, too," Raul admitted sheepishly. "So now I want to ask her to marry me and I thought of the circus."

"Of course you did." Alicia reached forward and touched his arm. She had a gooey look on her face. "Isn't it romantic, Tony?" She turned to him, smiling so widely he could see nearly all her teeth.

"Yes, but there are some practical considerations," he reminded her.

"Which we'll overcome."

"I don't see—"

"Raul, I think your proposal is a wonderful idea and I'm so glad you've agreed to share it with

'Hartson Flowers' viewers. Now, let me check my notes.''

The sappy look was gone as she consulted her papers. Tony was gratified that Alicia wasn't so lost in the romance of the situation that she had forgotten their main concern.

"Did you get the parade permit?"

"Yes." Raul jumped up and retrieved a paper from the kitchen table. "And the ring." He brought both over to Alicia.

"May I?" She picked up the velvet box.

Grinning, Raul gestured for her to open it.

She did, oohing and aahing as though it was the Hope diamond.

It was a modest ring. Very modest.

Tony approved. At least the young man hadn't tried to beggar himself or begin his married life in debt for a piece of jewelry.

"The middle diamond is surrounded by eight little ones." Raul pointed. "One for each year I've known Lillie."

"Ohhh." Alicia looked like she was ready to melt into a puddle or cry. Or both.

"Did you want to ask about the circus details?" Tony prodded.

But she either forgot about the street problem or intended to ignore it because she made an appointment for the following morning to meet with the circus personnel. Tony couldn't believe it, but rather than take over the way he wanted to, he waited until they were in the car and driving toward the motel before finally mentioning the subject.

"Please explain why you encouraged that young man," he demanded, conscious of sounding harsher than he'd intended.

"What do you mean? Isn't that the most romantic story you've ever heard?"

"I don't care how romantic it is. Why didn't you tell him a circus parade is impossible?"

"Because it isn't. He's got the permit."

"How—" Tony broke off. The world had gone crazy. Alicia had gone crazy. "I don't care what he's got. Elephants can't wander down that street."

"They won't be wandering. They have trainers."

"Suppose those trainers can't control them? Suppose the elephants take a few steps to one side? Think what they'd do to the yards. Think what they'd do to the *cars*. And 'Hartson Flowers' and Domenico Cable Productions would be held liable. We'd be sued for everything we've got."

"That's not going to happen," Alicia insisted. "You worry too much."

It was an unfortunate word choice. Hearing her say that particular phrase released all the frustration Tony'd been holding back. "You're exactly right—it's not going to happen."

He heard her draw a breath. "What are you saying?"

Tony stopped at a traffic light and took the opportunity to face her directly. "I'm saying we're *not* taping this proposal."

Her eyes narrowed. "It's not your decision. I'm in charge."

"Not anymore."

CHAPTER FOUR

ALICIA was extremely proud of herself. She did not throw an hysterical fit, however much she was entitled. Though she seethed inside, she maintained a cool, professional outer facade—until she reached the inside of her motel room. Even then, she was conscious that Tony was in the next room and would certainly hear her if she shouted out her frustration the way she wanted to.

She ran for the phone, then thought better of talking to Georgia while she was still furious with Tony. Georgia would get upset and that wouldn't be good for the babies.

After pounding on her pillow and the mattress for several minutes, Alicia felt calmer, but no less outraged.

Tony had no right to tell her what to do. No moral right anyway. After all this time, didn't he trust her? This would be the fourth Valentine special she and Georgia had produced. Couldn't he have some faith in their—*her* abilities and experience? He wouldn't even *listen* to her.

Alicia snatched the television remote from the nightstand and turned on the TV to the cable news channel, hoping the sound would muffle her conversation with Georgia. In spite of her intentions, Alicia didn't trust herself not to start ranting and raving.

"How did it go with Raul?" Georgia asked.

"It's the most romantic story!" And Alicia was determined to tape it in spite of Tony.

"Did he tell you about their trying out for the circus?"

"Yes." Alicia repeated her conversation with Raul, leaving out any references to Tony.

"So what does Tony think?"

Briefly, Alicia considered fudging the answer, but Georgia knew her too well. "He doesn't think it can be done because of the street."

Georgia laughed. "We'll show him."

"Okay, I'm all for that. How?" Alicia refused to tell her that Tony had taken over and canceled the taping. Georgia couldn't do anything about it and Alicia wasn't going to pay any attention to him anyway.

"If the street's small, then the circus parade will have to be small. Use baby animals."

Baby animals. Of course. Collapsing back onto the bed, Alicia closed her eyes, a wide smile on her face. "You are, as usual, brilliant. It's perfect. Assuming they have baby animals."

"They do. I've already checked."

She should have known Georgia would come up with something. After chatting about a few more points, Alicia hung up the phone. She felt immeasurably better. Even a little hungry.

There was a knock at her door. "Who is it?" she called, expecting one of the crew to answer. Since Brownsville was right on the border with Mexico, they'd talked about finding a great Mexican restaurant for dinner.

"Tony."

Well, there was an appetite killer. Dragging herself off the bed, Alicia took her time answering the door.

He stood in the doorway, tall and solemn. Even taller than she remembered, but that was probably because she'd kicked her shoes off. "Yes?"

"I wanted to discuss this second proposal with you." He was holding the report she'd given him.

"We haven't finished with the first one yet."

"Yes, we have. It's not doable."

Alicia hated it when people used the word "doable". "In whose opinion?" She was picking an argument when she'd tried to avoid arguing during the interminable drive from Houston and the meeting with Raul. Instead of telling him Georgia's suggestion, she'd chosen combative words just to see if she could get him to lose his temper. She needed the release of a good yelling match. One had been brewing between them for years.

"In any sane person's opinion," Tony replied. Obviously, he wasn't above a little inflammatory response, himself.

"That would be an unimaginative, uncreative, repressed sane person, wouldn't it?"

"It would be the sane person who's paying for it."

"Oh, please. You wouldn't have any money if we hadn't made it for you in the first place!" That was a wicked jab and she knew it.

Tony's eyes blazed, burning and dark at the same time. "Please keep your voice down."

At last, a reaction. Instead of being intimidated, Alicia found herself energized. She'd deliberately fueled his anger. If Tony felt anger, then he was also capable of feeling joy and passion. And then, maybe, he could understand why it was important to attempt to fulfill Raul Garza's dreams.

"How do you think 'Hartson Flowers' got to be so successful? Because we pushed," she said, answering her own question. "We never quit, never gave up as long as there was a chance we could make a segment work. And this one will work. I know it will." She waited for him to ask how.

"And afterward will you run a segment on all the lawsuits?"

"There aren't going to *be* any lawsuits."

A door slammed, drawing Tony's attention. "I'm not standing in a hallway and arguing with you about it."

"Then we'll go someplace else and argue about it." Leaving him in the doorway, she slipped on her shoes and slung her purse over her shoulder.

He was leaning against the wall, waiting for her when she emerged from her room. She'd half expected him to have stormed off, but storming off wasn't his style. Suppressing was his style.

"I'll check in with the guys." She knocked on the door across the hall.

"They've gone already," Tony said to her surprise. "They wanted to walk across the border and try a restaurant on the Matamoros side."

"And they didn't tell me?"

"Your phone line was busy."

They could have called me on the cell phone, she thought but didn't voice. She had a feeling they'd not wanted to eat dinner with Tony and knew she wouldn't snub him. *Thanks a lot, guys.* She'd been

saving up calories for a really good Mexican food
binge. Maybe tomorrow night.

"There's a coffee shop attached to the motel. We
can go there." He gestured to her purse. "Don't
you need your notebook?"

"Nope." *Since there's nothing new to discuss.*
They walked out into the balmy night air. Alicia
drew in a deep breath and smelled grasses and plants
in bloom. Growing things. "It doesn't even smell
like winter here."

"What does winter smell like?"

Alicia was glad Tony had apparently decided to
wait before resuming their argument. "You know
that cold, metallic smell? The wood smoke and
pine?"

He shook his head. "I'm a native Houstonian.
I don't know what cold smells like."

"Didn't you ever travel?"

"Not in winter. Except once in college, when I
went on a university-sponsored skiing trip to
Colorado."

Another piece of personal information. Alicia
found herself squirreling it away with the other
nuggets he'd dropped. "Well, what was that like?"

"Cold and wet. I didn't have the right kind of
clothes." They arrived at the coffee shop and he
held open the door for her. "I didn't know how to
ski anyway."

"Then why did you go?"

"The girl I was dating at the time wanted to go,
so I said I would go with her."

A waitress showed them to a booth.

As she slid across the red vinyl seat, Alicia
grappled with the image of Tony dating—specifi-

cally what had happened to the relationship. She would have asked more questions, but Tony immediately began to study the laminated menu.

Alicia decided on a salad. No sense in wasting the calories here when she could feast tomorrow night. Besides, they had an argument to finish.

"Is that all you're having?" Tony asked when the waitress came to take their orders.

"I'll make up for it at breakfast," she responded, then added, "Don't forget we're meeting with the circus people at nine."

Tony ordered a hamburger before taking Alicia's bait. "At nine, we're going to be on the road to Austin."

"You can go to Austin tomorrow. I'm staying here."

She watched his chest rise and fall. His eyes no longer blazed, but Alicia knew he was angry. "I have already explained that we will not be taping here."

"And I've explained that it isn't your decision." His eyes widened slightly and Alicia continued, "Everyone who appears on camera signs a release."

"Historically, those don't hold up in court. Besides, I'm concerned about liability from the Oakwood residents more than I am Raul and his girlfriend."

"Why won't you even listen? We've done some of the most incredible stories. This one will be great. All the parts are there." She raised her hand and began ticking off the reasons on her fingers. "We have childhood sweethearts, we have a circus—how many people wanted to run away with the circus at some point in their lives?—and we have two people in love. What more do you need?''

''How about an extra two lanes on that street?''

He was impossible. Alicia stood, no longer hungry and no longer spoiling for a fight. ''We don't need the extra lanes. And if you want to find out why, stick around.''

''I have no intention of allowing you—''

''This is not a matter of your *allowing* anything. This is my show and my decision. You are supposed to be assisting me, not pulling rank!'' In poking the embers of Tony's anger, she'd ignited her own.

''Be at the car by nine o'clock.''

''By nine o'clock, I'll be at the circus!'' Alicia was conscious of drawing the stares of other diners. She didn't care.

''Not if you want to continue taping this show.''

''Excuse me? *You're* the one who wanted us to proceed with the Valentine special as planned.''

Tony opened his mouth, then apparently changed his mind about what he'd been going to say. ''It...won't...work.'' Each word was quiet and distinct.

Alicia answered him in kind. ''Yes...it...will.''

''Uh, ma'am?'' The waitress stood behind her with a laden tray. ''I'm ready to serve.''

Alicia glanced from the tray to Tony, then turned and strode out of the coffee shop before she could succumb to the overwhelming desire to dump her dinner on Tony's head.

At eight-thirty the next morning, Alicia was nervous. She was nervous because of the way she'd left Tony the night before—not staying to eat dinner with him. Childish to stomp off, but that's what she'd done.

It was also childish not to tell him about using baby animals, and she didn't know why she hadn't except that she'd wanted him to trust her.

Should she knock on his door now and remind him that they had to leave? She was taking the car, so he wouldn't be able to drive off at nine.

She closed the door to her room loudly, then hesitated, hoping he'd open his door. When he didn't, she started down the hallway, then abruptly pivoted. This was ridiculous. He was supposed to be assisting her. Standing directly in front of his door, she raised her hand to knock.

The door swung inward.

Alicia yelped, then backed up awkwardly, at a loss for words. "I—I'm leaving now."

"Yes." He closed his door, then peered at her. "Stop looking at me as though I'm going to bodily haul you off."

"I'm not entirely certain what you're going to do."

"I believe we have an appointment at a circus."

The "we" part bothered her. "Well, last I heard, you wanted to go to Austin. That would have been difficult since I'll be driving the car." If she didn't know better, she could have sworn a smug expression crossed his face.

"With what, these?" Tony dangled the keys in front of her face.

"No, with these." Alicia dangled her own set back at him.

"Well, well." He pocketed his set. "Where did you get those?"

"I leave an extra set with one of the crew in case I lock mine in the car."

"Has that ever happened?"

"Unfortunately, yes. I get distracted sometimes."

"I imagine you do," he murmured.

As they walked to the parking lot, Alicia tried to ascertain Tony's mood. He didn't appear to be angry or resigned. Just neutral. Surely he felt *something* and it was driving her nuts trying to figure out what.

"Baby animals." Tony approached Alicia as she directed the crew to tape background material on the circus grounds.

"Yes, including a cute and highly photogenic baby elephant, which Lillie will ride."

"You could have told me."

Alicia ran a microphone cord down the sleeve of her red blazer. She'd be wearing red and hot pink on camera for the entire Valentine special. "You could have asked."

"You knew my objections."

She clipped the cord to the lapel mike. "And you knew my track record." Gazing up at him, she saw the tightness to his features that she now recognized as anger. Too bad. She had more of a right to be angry than he did. He hadn't apologized for doubting her or anything. "Do you have anything else to say? I'm taping commentary now."

"Yes, I do have something to say." He gestured to her red blazer and white wool pants. "You look like a giant candy cane." Then he walked off.

Alicia's jaw grew slack. "These are Valentine colors!"

Tony kept walking.

Alicia turned to the cameraman. "Jake, waist up only in the frame, okay?"

Tomorrow, she'd wear black pants. The white wool was itchy in this heat anyway.

"I'm Alicia Hartson here with Raul Garza who is about to propose to his longtime love, Lillie Patterson. How did you two meet, Raul?"

Alicia tilted the microphone toward Raul. This was the second time they'd taped Raul's portion of the program. He was so nervous, Alicia was afraid they'd have to tape a third time in order to splice together a decent interview.

She wondered how Tony was faring. He and the second cameraman were located at the beginning of Lillie Patterson's street. Alicia and her crewman would follow Raul. Tony was to capture Lillie's reaction.

The sound tech was hiding in the bushes at Lillie's house, ready to alert them if she left. Lillie was a hairdresser, and Wednesday was her day off. Raul, who worked as a deliveryman, had mentioned that he might drop by, but was afraid to make any definite plans in case Lillie became suspicious.

Clowns, animals and various circus vehicles were assembling at a grocery store parking lot just around the corner. As soon as Raul finished his interview, he and Alicia would join them.

"So this is your dream come true in more ways than one, isn't it?" Alicia asked, referring to Raul's motorcycle attire.

"Yes," he said with a shy eagerness.

"Let's go, then." Alicia signaled for the camera to follow, as Raul, in his silver-spangled biker outfit, gunned the engine and roared down the road. "He's going too fast!" Alicia jumped in the "Hartson Flowers" van. "Jake, keep taping!" She was driving. Georgia was going to have fun writing narrative for this.

They sped through the Brownsville streets but were caught by one too many red lights.

"Lost him," the cameraman said and raised the van window.

"I'm not surprised." Alicia hoped Tony was getting some good footage.

She arrived at the parking lot to find ponies, dogs, and one toothless, muzzled gray tiger, which Tony was taping. He beckoned to Alicia.

"This tiger is retired," Tony told her. "They thought he'd enjoy one more parade. Look." He pointed as the handler put a sequined ruff over the tiger's head. "He's holding still. You can tell he's an old pro."

"Oh, how sweet!" As she watched, the tiger allowed the ruff to be fastened before tossing its head with majestic haughtiness.

"Go talk to the handler," Tony urged. "Get some tape."

It was a good idea. Alicia did so. They'd already covered the animal park where the retired circus animals lived out their lives. Sensing a future segment, Alicia had devoted most of yesterday afternoon taping around the park.

When she finished, she approached Tony. "They're ready," he told her.

Alicia drew a deep breath. The next hour would determine how successful this segment would be. "Okay, you follow Raul. Be sure you remind him to get down on one knee and open the ring box."

"What if he doesn't want to?"

Alicia stared at him. "Why wouldn't he want to?"

"Because it's corny."

"It's romantic."

"It's a cliché."

Alicia pitied the poor woman Tony would propose to. "Our viewers expect it. Every proposal we've shown has been that way. Except the sky divers."

Tony looked as though he wanted to argue, but the circus music began blaring from a loudspeaker attached to a brightly painted wooden cart the clowns were riding in. Shaking his head, he headed toward Raul.

Alicia and her cameraman, Jake, headed for Lillie's house. Cars had been cleared from the streets and neighbors were watching from their yards. The third crewman had passed out pom-poms and balloons.

The visuals were great. The weather was perfect. Now for the difficult part. Filming marriage proposals was exciting because of the element of the unexpected. Lillie could turn him down. Or freeze when she saw the cameras. Alicia would try to be unobtrusive, but she still had to get a good shot.

Drums sounded in the distance and the clown cart with the loudspeaker rounded the corner. The morning sun glinted off thousands of sequins. Warm gulf breezes fluttered feathers. Lillie's neighbors, who were in on the secret, stood in their front yards and cheered.

Alicia and her cameraman were positioned by the front door and she felt her pulse quicken in anticipation.

"She *is* at home, isn't she?" an anxious Alicia verified with Jake.

He nodded and grinned, well used to her nervous last-minute questions.

"Better let me hold the costume." Alicia had borrowed a cape and feathered tiara for Lillie to wear.

Raul was now visible, leading the parade. Behind him lumbered the baby elephant.

"Oh, look, how cute!" Alicia cooed. Tony better be getting this on tape. There was a sparkling flash as the sunlight caught Raul's silver biker costume. "I hope the glare doesn't skew the light readings too much."

"Nah. It'll be fine."

The music grew louder. From her vantage point, she tried to see into the house. Surely Lillie could hear the parade. When was she coming out? Alicia wished she had a person she could send around to the back of the house. Motioning her crew to remain, Alicia backed up until she could see the second-story window. Was that a hand at the curtain? "I think she's coming."

Jake swiveled the camera toward the front door.

Raul pulled his motorcycle to a stop in front of Lillie's house. The elephant and his handlers stopped, too. As planned, the rest of the circus personnel continued to the end of the street where they would turn around and come back. If all went well, they'd arrive about the time Raul proposed and he and Lillie would join the parade.

Where was Lillie? Just as Alicia was about to break down the front door and drag Lillie Patterson out by her hair, the door opened and a petite, angelic-looking blonde with clouds of curly hair emerged from the house.

She hesitated, noticing Alicia and the camera. "Raul?"

"It's me, Lillie." His voice cracked.

"What is all this?"

He climbed off the motorcycle, his legs visibly shaking. Alicia hoped Tony's cameraman was cropping this. Or maybe not. Men who shook with the emotion of the moment were so endearing.

"Remember how we always wanted to be in the circus?" Raul gestured behind him.

"Oh, Raul."

At that moment, Alicia relaxed. Lillie was regarding Raul with a look of such love and tenderness that Alicia knew an acceptance was forthcoming. She stepped forward and wrapped a startled Lillie in a pink-and-silver sequined cape—more great visuals—and fastened the tiara on her head. Then she stood back to let the drama unfold.

Tony and his cameraman were in place. The circus parade had begun to double back.

Raul looked at Alicia and she smiled and nodded. He dropped to one knee.

"Oh, my God!" Lillie squealed and clapped her hands over her mouth.

"Lillie, I've loved you since we were children," Raul began.

Alicia got goose bumps.

"And since we were children we've had a dream."

Lillie began to cry softly. So did Alicia.

The sound tech repositioned the microphone.

"Today, I'm making our childhood dream come true and I hope you make my adult dream come true." With trembling hands, Raul fumbled with a zippered pocket before bringing out the velvet ring box. He pried it open.

"Oh, Raul." Lillie's hands still covered her mouth.

"Lillie, this ring has nine diamonds, one for each year I've known you." He gazed at her with such longing that had he proposed to Alicia in that moment, *she* would have accepted. "And one for each year I've loved you. Will you marry me?"

Alicia pressed her knuckles against her mouth to stifle a sob. It didn't matter how many proposals she witnessed, she teared up at each one.

Lillie hiccuped a yes and collapsed against Raul's shoulder. Unfortunately, her head was turned away from Alicia. Blinking back tears, she frantically signaled Tony to tape Raul putting the ring on Lillie's finger.

Tony gave her a thumbs-up sign.

Alicia maneuvered her cameraman out of Tony's frame.

The newly engaged couple kissed, accompanied by cheers from the neighbors and the return of the circus parade.

After that, Lillie was escorted to the elephant and the trainers helped her sit on his back. Raul revved up his motorcycle and the parade continued down the street.

"Is that a wrap?" Tony called. "I think we've got enough parade shots."

"I agree." Alicia dabbed at her eyes.

Tony approached her. "Hey, congratulations." He grinned and shook his head. "That was great. I've got to hand it to you. I didn't think you could pull this one off." He stared after the happy couple before turning back to her.

Alicia was staring at him. *He was smiling*. He'd even chuckled. Not quite a laugh, but definitely a sound of amusement. He should laugh more often. It made him more human and infinitely more attractive.

"What?" He'd noticed her stare.

"Uh, does my mascara look okay? It should. It's waterproof," she babbled.

Tony tilted her chin upward and studied her face. His scrutiny was more thorough than Alicia had expected and she was very aware of his nearness and the cool touch of his fingers against her warming face.

One finger brushed at her cheek. "The mascara's okay, but you might touch up the blush." He drew his fingers away.

Alicia could still feel the path they'd traced over her skin. This wouldn't do. Nodding, she dabbed at her eyes again. "I'll put on more when I'm sure I've finished crying."

"Why are you crying? I thought you'd be thrilled. Raul and Lillie are engaged and we got the whole thing on tape—just the way you wanted. One down, two to go."

"It was all so romantic. Did you hear the part about the dreams?" Alicia's eyes filled again. "That was so romantic."

He smiled. "So you've said."

"Well, it was." She pulled another tissue from her pocket.

Tony drew his brows together, looking more like the old Tony. "Do you always cry?"

"Pretty much." Alicia blew her nose. "That's how I know I've got a good proposal segment."

At that, Tony laughed. A real laugh. An out-loud laugh. "Then this one must be great."

CHAPTER FIVE

"HI." ALICIA smiled into the camera, hoping the wind would die down long enough for her to finish taping. "Behind me—" she turned and gestured off into the distance "—is beautiful Austin, the state capital of Texas. And this is where our next proposal will take place."

She paused to allow Jake to pan the vista spread before them. They were parked at a scenic overlook right outside the city. Cars and trucks whizzed past on the highway, making it difficult for Alicia to get a complete take in one shot.

"But instead of the modern city you see here, we're going to transport you to the medieval times of knights on white horses, kings, queens and fair maidens." She dropped her mike. "How was that?"

"Sounded great," Tony said. "The traffic cooperated. The sun came out just when Jake panned, though. It'll look like we spliced."

"Think we should try again?" Alicia checked her appearance in the equipment van's side mirror. A little windblown, but not too bad. The temperature was mild, but with the wind, it was chilly. She'd be glad to get back into the car.

"Let me check the traffic." Tony jogged past the crest of the hill. "There's an eighteen-wheeler with several cars behind it," he called. "When they pass, you'll have a break."

"Okay." Alicia looked skyward. "Jake, let's try it from over here. I don't want to squint into the sun." Clearing her throat and flexing her arms, Alicia waited until the truck roared past before going through her spiel again. The breeze had picked up and she could feel it moving her hair, so she wasn't certain which take she'd prefer. "Good?" she asked when she'd finished.

"Great," Tony answered.

Alicia wanted to shake him. They were being so polite and so cooperative with each other. Tony deferred to her on every single little detail. It was about to drive her nuts. She, on the other hand, asked his opinion on every single little detail, which she could tell irritated him. And she planned to continue.

It was a contest to see who would crack first.

Why were they doing this to each other?

After the first proposal's success, they should be more comfortable with each other. Tony had unbent, proving that he could. Alicia had demonstrated her competence—not that she should have had to.

She knew the exaggerated politeness between them wasn't her imagination. She'd caught the looks the crew gave them and how the three men managed to be elsewhere whenever Tony and Alicia were together.

Shrugging off the pink jacket, Alicia hung it on a hanger and hooked it in the back of the car. "Why don't we go directly to the restaurant, so our outdoor shots will match this light?" She turned to Tony with a smile, wishing she hadn't phrased her request as a question. She wanted to go to

Camelot Castle now, even though her schedule
called for a visit with the prospective groom. She'd
made the schedule; she could change the schedule.
She didn't need Tony's approval or permission.

"That's a great idea," he said.

Alicia gritted her teeth. Everything she'd said or
done had been "great". Couldn't he come up with
another adjective?

"If you see a problem with that, just say so."

He merged into the highway traffic. "I told you
it sounded great."

"Yet you know it isn't on the schedule."

"You must have your reasons."

"I do. The lighting. I told you."

"And I said it sounded great."

"If it didn't sound great, would you tell me?"

Tony didn't answer immediately. "The last time
I expressed my opinion, I was very firmly put in
my place."

Oh, forever more. Alicia loosened her shoulder
belt so she could swivel and face him. "Is this still
about the circus parade?"

He didn't answer.

"You resent the fact that everything worked out,
don't you?"

"What is there to resent? The parade was
a . . . roaring success, as they say."

"Yes, it was." She waited for him to continue.

At last, he did. "You proved that my input was
not needed, so I'm simply staying out of your way."

The male ego was an astonishing thing. It crept
up at the most unlikely times in the most unlikely
men. With great forbearance, Alicia refrained from

strangling Tony. "If I recall," she mused sweetly, "you weren't inputting, you were squashing."

He drew a long breath and his hands flexed on the steering wheel. "I'll admit to expressing strong opinions." He slid a quick glance at her. "Since you're a professional, I assumed I wouldn't have to constantly moderate my language."

He was intimating that it was her fault! Alicia was speechless.

"If you'd told me about the baby elephant and the other animals, then we could have avoided a lot of strife."

"If you'd acted as if you'd have listened to me, I might have told you!" she snapped, then turned to face the road. "And here I thought you were human," she grumbled, more loudly than she'd intended, but not sorry he'd heard.

"I've found that women launch personal attacks during disagreements. Men keep to the facts. That's why we can disagree and still remain friends."

He sounded so smugly superior. Alicia's fingers curled into the car's upholstery. "We weren't disagreeing. *You* decided to take over. If I'd been a man, you wouldn't have pulled that stunt."

Tony groaned. "Do *not* turn this into a battle of the sexes."

"*I* didn't!"

"Can you honestly say you're treating me as you would a woman?"

It was Alicia's turn to sound smug. "Absolutely not. If you were a woman, I'd be driving."

Tony muttered something under his breath and pulled off the road. "So drive!"

Alicia was out of the car like a shot. The "Hartson Flowers" van pulled in behind them. "Everything's okay," she called, motioning them on. She marched around the rear of the car.

"We're okay," Tony echoed as they crossed paths.

"Don't you mean *great*?" Alicia snarled, stepping into the driver's side.

They both slammed the car doors and jerked at their shoulder harnesses, shoving them at the holders in the center of the car seat at the same time. Somehow, they got the straps tangled and twisted together. Alicia's buckle was fastened in Tony's slot and it wouldn't release. She yanked at it in frustration until she noticed that Tony's shoulders were shaking. Within seconds, his laughter broke though.

"Listen to us." He leaned his head back, still laughing. "We sound like a couple of kids."

With a weak pull on the tangled seat belt, Alicia gave in to her own laughter. So what if the first time she'd actually heard him let loose and laugh it was at her own expense? She didn't know how long they sat on the side of the road and laughed, but every time they tried to untangle the seat belts, it set them off again.

"I'll hold the button, you pull," Tony finally said.

Giggling, Alicia did so and was freed. She sank against the seat, not immediately driving off. Their laughter had cleared the air. "We do sound pretty juvenile, don't we?"

Tony rubbed his chin. "Did you and Georgia ever argue like that?"

"No." Alicia shook her head. "But we think a lot alike." She looked over at him. "You and I don't think alike."

He half smiled. "No."

"You said men can disagree and still be friends. Maybe that's why we don't get along. We're not friends." *But you don't want to be friends*, an inner voice whispered. *You want to be more.* Alicia silenced it. She most certainly did *not* want to be more. In fact, she wasn't sure about trying to be Tony's friend.

"Are you saying you want us to be friends?" he asked, his voice skeptical.

"I don't know you well enough to know whether I want to be your friend or not," she said, speaking with more truth than was perhaps wise. "Nobody knows much about you."

He raised his eyebrows. "I was unaware that my private life was the cause of such curiosity and discussion."

"There you are getting all huffy." Alicia made a face before sitting up and putting the car in gear. "You don't want anybody to get to know you, do you?"

She stomped on the accelerator and joined the highway traffic.

"Why do you say that? Because I don't spill my guts by the office watercooler?" Tony hated being driven by other people, especially when the driver then proceeded to interrogate him.

"You don't have to spill your guts, but a little leaking wouldn't hurt. You spend the entire day cooped up in your office. People hardly see you."

"It appears that I have less free time than some others."

Alicia gestured with her hands, too. He wished she'd keep them on the steering wheel. She signaled a lane change. "So what do you do with your time?"

"I *work*."

"That wasn't what I meant." Alicia shook her head. "Look in my notebook for the directions to that restaurant, would you? There's a highway interchange coming up and I can't remember which road to take." As he flipped through her scrawlings looking for anything that appeared to be directions, she continued, "So what do you do when you're not at work?"

He *thought* about work. He took paperwork home with him. Occasionally, he'd watch a little television. He visited his parents every Friday and sometimes on Sunday for Mass. It all sounded mundane, now that he thought about it. Drab. Nothing about his life would interest a woman like Alicia in the slightest.

What did *she* do when she wasn't at work? He thought about asking her, but didn't. She talked enough without his encouraging her. He'd undoubtedly learn everything there was to know about her before they returned to Houston.

At last he found the directions—neatly printed— and read them to her, thus avoiding answering her question.

He hoped she'd talk about the upcoming proposal.

But no. "So, you're not married. Are you seeing anyone? Got a roommate?"

"No."

"You live alone." She nodded. "I live alone."

That surprised him. "I would have thought you wouldn't like living alone."

"At first I didn't, but now I like the quiet. I recharge in the quiet."

Tony gazed at her. The woman next to him was the most vital, exhaustingly energetic woman he'd ever met. That she craved quiet as he did intrigued him.

"Do you have any pets?" she asked.

"No. It wouldn't be fair to them since I work such long hours."

"Hey. You voluntarily expanded on a yes-or-no question. That's progress." She sent an approving smile his way. "I used to have a cat, but I asked my across-the-hall neighbor to keep her so many times, the cat got confused about who her owner was. She still lives with my neighbor."

"I'm sorry."

"I didn't mind."

But he thought she did.

"So, tell me how you started Domenico Cable Productions."

"That's not a yes-or-no question."

She grinned. "I figured you were ready for the big time."

Tony made a show of checking his watch. "How long until we get to the Camelot Castle?"

"It's in the hills on the other side of town. You've got plenty of time. Relax and talk."

Tony couldn't remember the last time someone had asked him how he got started in the business. Probably during that interview with the entrepreneurial magazine, which this conversation was suspiciously resembling. Alicia was undoubtedly fishing for a future story. He shouldn't encourage her, yet he found he wanted to tell her. "I suppose the beginning was a summer job that got out of hand."

She laughed. "I'll say."

"My father is a musician. He teaches a little and he plays a little."

"What instrument?"

"Violin and viola. He plays in a string quartet. They hire themselves out for weddings and so forth. One summer, I was home from college for about six weeks and I couldn't find a short-term job. Pop's quartet wanted me to videotape them so they'd have something to send people who were interested in hiring them. I found that I really liked being behind the camera. I enjoyed the whole process."

"Do you miss it?"

"Yes," he admitted quietly, "I do." In fact, until he'd taped Raul yesterday, he'd not realized how much he missed being in the field. "I was good."

"You still are. I saw the footage."

"Yeah?" He smiled.

"Yes, To-ny," she said in a singsong voice. "You've still got it."

He chuckled, almost embarrassed by the pleasure her words brought him. It had been years since he retired from dragging a crew around. At the very modest start of Domenico Cable Productions, Tony had handled everything himself. As soon as he could, he hired a fellow college student to carry equipment and set up lights. He taped weddings, birthdays, funerals, Bar Mitzvahs, graduations,

christenings—anything people wanted to remember. Then he taped job seekers for a segment
he marketed to local television stations.

His first studio was the second bedroom in a two-
bedroom apartment. Soon, he hired another
person. Then another. When his business outgrew
the bedroom, he leased his first commercial office
space.

They were on the outskirts of Austin and the
highway begin to climb and twist. Alicia handled
the car with enough competence that Tony quit
watching the speedometer.

"What happened after you taped your father?
You hire yourself out to videotape weddings?"

"Not immediately." Tony was more comfortable
talking with her now. "The quartet offered me a
commission for each job I could get them. I walked
that tape all over town."

"*That's* how you got into the marketing end."
Alicia nodded as though she now had some missing
piece of information. "You were just as good at
that, weren't you?"

He shrugged. "I made more money that summer
than I ever had before." So had his father.

"Then what?"

The questions kept coming and he figured they
would until he asked her to stop. "Then I went back
to school and changed my major. I quit when I
realized I knew more than the professors."

"You were certainly sure of yourself."

"Yes and no. The industry was so new we were
all learning at the same time. The cable market was
booming and I wanted to get in on it. Two more

years in school and I might have missed my opportunity.''

It had been the one time his parents' impracticality had sustained him. Instead of encouraging him to remain in school, they'd insisted he follow his dream. Funny, he'd forgotten all about that.

As they'd been talking, the terrain had changed. They were climbing the hills surrounding Austin. When they rounded one bend, Tony caught a glimpse of a turret with colorful flags flying from it. ''Did you see that? I'll bet that's the restaurant.''

''I'll bet you're right. Keep an eye out for the turn.''

''I will.'' He hesitated. ''Could I ask you a question without your getting defensive?''

''If you'll listen to the answer without getting dictatorial.''

Fair enough. ''Why did you allow an extra day for this proposal? It seems fairly innocuous.''

''Weather, and because there are so many people involved.''

''More than the circus?''

Alicia nodded. ''The circus was just doing what they always do. This time, we've got costumes and her sorority sisters and his fraternity brothers and parents flying in and so on. Georgia and I have a rule. One extra day for every dozen people.''

''Will the budget cover everything?'' He knew the budgeted amount and it appeared ''Hartson Flowers'' was being overly generous.

She flicked a glance toward him. ''We're picking up a large chunk of the tab,'' she admitted. ''But not everything.''

To Tony, it sounded like a couple of college kids were throwing a party at the program's expense. "I hope you nailed down the particulars." And set limits. But he'd voiced his objections. Any further discussion would irritate Alicia. He'd have to sit back and see how this one unfolded.

Alicia was dying to continue questioning Tony, but knew better than to push it.

His story of how he got started in the business told her he had vision and determination. He still had the determination, but what had happened to the vision? Dropping out of school and starting a company at such a young age was not a conservative move. What had changed him from the risk taker he'd been not that long ago?

The more she pried out of him, the more intrigued she became. Unfortunately, they'd arrived at the Camelot Castle medieval restaurant, and further revelations from Tony would have to wait.

Parking the car, Alicia threw open the door and gazed at the sight before them. "A moat! A drawbridge and a moat, can you believe it?"

Tony apparently didn't share her excitement, but she wasn't really surprised. Directing the camera crew to tape background filler, Alicia prepared for the second part of the introduction.

The restaurant itself was on a cliff, and Lake Travis glistened in the background. "I bet this place is fabulous at night," she said and gave Tony the hand mike to hold.

"I suppose you'll use this view for your stand-up background?" he asked.

"No kidding!" Alicia unhooked her pink jacket, put it on and touched up her makeup.

Tony walked toward the drawbridge, gesturing for the crew to follow him. Alicia watched him for a moment, then reviewed her notes. Georgia had written the introduction to the segment when all they'd seen was a brochure featuring the restaurant. Alicia thought the speech was a little adjective-laden, but frankly, the brochure couldn't do the restaurant justice. Now, she considered the speech subdued, if anything.

They'd parked in the lot beneath a guard tower, where the restaurant patrons checked in. A proclamation in hard-to-read medieval type announced that after gaining admittance, guests could either walk across the bridge or be transported by cart and horse. For an extra charge, private chairs were available.

Alicia made notes. There was only one snag that she could foresee. The groom, one Granger "Whitey" Whitfield II, dressed in full armor, planned to capture his maiden, Amber Nicole Hewlet, on a white horse and ride off with her to this castle.

Unfortunately, fifteen miles of winding open highway separated Amber's sorority house near the University of Texas campus and Camelot Castle. There was no way Whitey could ride the horse that distance.

Alicia tapped her pencil against her notebook. She and Georgia liked to present the proposals truthfully, but in this case, some judicious editing would be appropriate—like cutting from the time Whitey rode off with Amber to his arrival here at the castle. The important part would happen inside anyway, when Amber would be dressed, as well as the rest of the guests, in a medieval costume and led to a banquet attended by her parents and sorority sisters and Whitey's fraternity brothers. The costume rental fees had been a huge part of the total budget for the Valentine special, but Georgia and Alicia had been charmed by the scope of the fantasy.

The segment was due to be filmed on Sunday, when the restaurant was normally closed. Fortunately, Whitey's parents were paying for the meal. Even so, Alicia knew why Tony was concerned. This would be one of their most romantic—but costly— proposals yet. If all went well, women viewers would be enthralled. And if it didn't...

Alicia buttoned her jacket. If this segment didn't work, she'd be asking Tony for more money. The prospect was too horrible to contemplate.

Plastering on her professional television smile, Alicia raised the microphone to her mouth. "Behind me—" she gestured '—Camelot Castle..."

CHAPTER SIX

"SOMETHING'S wrong." Alicia stared at the activity inside Amber's sorority house. "I feel it." She tapped her chest. "Here."

"What makes you think that?" Tony kept his voice light, but seeing Alicia without the customary smile on her face made him wary. They'd spent the past two days taping background in preparation for tomorrow's proposal sequence and Alicia's enthusiasm had noticeably waned.

"There's too much going on." She pointed to the young women weaving flowers into head-dresses. Two of Whitey's friends argued over whose legs looked better in the tights their costumes required.

"So?" Tony signaled his cameraman to take a break. "Amber's mother has taken her shopping. She won't see any of this."

"What if she suspects something anyway?" Grasping his arm, Alicia urged him outside. "Whitey wrote to us right after Thanksgiving. Half the sorority house is over decorating the banquet hall. They've been planning the layout for weeks. The rest are obsessing with the costumes. How could they not have let something slip?"

Privately, Tony thought Alicia and Georgia should have considered that possibility before now. "She's expecting a fraternity party." Tony glanced down at Alicia just as they stepped from the shadow

91

of the huge oak tree and the sunlight struck her hair.

He paused to admire the golden strands. He'd caught himself noticing Alicia's appearance several times in the past few days and his attention drifted away from what she was saying.

He was going to have to stop that. She'd be furious if he said, "Sorry, I wasn't paying attention because I was watching your eyes or your mouth or the way you move your hands when you speak." And he couldn't figure out why he'd become fascinated with such things about a woman he'd known for several years—a woman he thought he disliked. A woman whose comfortable prettiness was overshadowed by her partner's stunning beauty.

Alicia gestured with her hand. Tony had noticed that she had to fight the habit when she was on camera. One hand gripped the microphone and the other held a clipboard or stayed in her pocket. "Wouldn't Amber expect to be helping with the party like everyone else? Instead, her mother flies in to take her shopping for a dress. Does her mother always do that? And her parents weren't even supposed to contact her ahead of time." Alicia frowned.

Concerned that Alicia's voice was carrying, Tony indicated they should head toward the equipment van and lightly touched the small of her back. "Her mother probably made up a plausible excuse for visiting."

"Yes, I realize that." Alicia ran her fingers through her hair as they walked. Alicia messing up her hair before going on camera was not a good sign. "This has become a slick production. *Her* parents flew here. *His* parents flew here. They're throwing a dinner party for sixty." She audibly exhaled. "Either Whitey's very sure of Amber's response—or he's already proposed."

"Would that be so terrible?"

"Yes!" Alicia regarded him as if he'd spouted blasphemy.

Tony felt that their discussion was irrelevant. Good TV was the only important thing. "Aren't all your proposers fairly certain they'll be accepted?"

"I hope so," she answered.

"Then I don't get it." And he wasn't loath to make the admission, either. Alicia had good instincts and he respected that, but he was weary of this constant speculation.

"Okay, I'll try to explain." They'd reached the van and Alicia thought for a moment. "When we capture an unexpected proposal, we get fresh emotions. Genuine and unrehearsed emotions. The audience responds because most of them have felt those same emotions before. They're reliving them." She gazed toward the sorority house. "This is all too staged."

"All right, say it is. What do you want to do?" he asked.

Her jaw hardened. "I say we confront Whitey."

"Why? Presumably, he knows the secrecy rule."

"Oh, yes."

Tony tried very hard not to think of all the money wasted if they didn't use the Camelot Castle proposal. "If you confront Whitey, then he'll either lie and say Amber doesn't know—technically, she might not—or he'll tell the truth and risk humiliation in front of his parents and peers when you cancel. What do *you* think he'll say?''

Alicia made a face. "I'm not saying *he* told her. Maybe her mother told her. I just don't have a good feeling.'' She tossed her notebook into the van. "This proposal isn't going to work.''

"I have a headache,'' Tony muttered, leaning against the van door.

"Do you want aspirin?'' She reached for her purse.

"No, I don't want aspirin! I want you to tape the proposal and stop this endless speculation about whether or not Amber will be surprised.'' And he would prefer that Alicia not argue with him about it. But he knew she would.

"The surprise is what makes it romantic!'' Sighing, Alicia waved to the crew. "We leave in five minutes!'' The guys were flirting with the college women and didn't notice—or ignored—her.

Tony put two fingers in his mouth, let loose with a piercing whistle and got their attention. He held up five fingers and got a thumbs-up in return.

The back door of the van was open and Alicia sat on the fender. "It could have been so good.'' Her frown stopped just short of being a pout.

If she and Georgia dissected every segment like this, he was surprised they accomplished anything. Tony joined her on the fender. "It'll still be romantic. Nothing has changed. And in front of all their friends and their parents, there'll be plenty of unrehearsed, genuine emotion.''

Alicia shook her head. "It'll be contrived.''

Tony looked skyward, hoping for patience. "All these elaborate proposals are contrived. If two people are in love, they don't need this extra stuff."

"But the extra 'stuff' is what makes it romantic," she insisted and crossed her arms.

Tony looked at her. "I thought love was what made it romantic."

"Well, yes." Alicia shivered and Tony immediately shrugged out of his leather jacket and put it around her shoulders. "Here, we can share." Scooting close, she opened up the jacket for him to put over his shoulder and casually leaned against him.

Tony stiffened involuntarily at her touch and deliberately forced himself to relax. She seemed so matter-of-fact about being this close to him that he should be the same. Still, he noticed that his arm curved naturally around her, as though she were made to fit in just that spot.

Alicia felt much tinier than she looked. He knew she kept herself slender for the camera, but he could feel the bones in her shoulder. The implied fragility stirred his protective instincts. Without analyzing what he was doing, he shifted slightly so she settled more firmly against him.

"But I also think men use that love-is-enough sentiment to avoid going to any effort to win a woman," she was saying.

Tony struggled to pick up the thread of their conversation. "What's this winning part? I thought modern women wanted to be equal partners."

"Can't we be equal partners and have romance, too?" She snuggled closer.

Tony was getting used to the feel of her against his chest. He was beginning to *like* the feel of her against his chest. "Is this what romance means to you? Thousands of dollars spent on costumes and props and your every move being recorded by a camera crew? That's not love. That's showing off."

"Romance doesn't have to be expensive or elaborate," she retorted.

"Oh, sure! That's why you're taping these simple, inexpensive, but heartfelt proposals, right?" Couldn't she see how hypocritical she was being?

"This is different. This is fantasy." She looked up at him and he was startled by what a clear blue her eyes were. Clear and direct, not clouded by secrets. She believed every word she was speaking.

"Fantasy," he repeated. "And simple romance would be ... ?"

"Romance is the extra effort men and women go through to please each other," she said. "To show that the person they love is important to them."

"And you don't think asking someone to get married is an indication of importance?"

"Importance, yes, being cherished, no."

"Now you want to be cherished, too?" Hopeless. She and all women like her were utterly hopeless. "It's like you want every day to be Valentine's Day."

Alicia nodded, her hair tickling his chin. He inhaled, liking the scent of her shampoo.

"The man I'll fall in love with is the type of man who'll write me love letters, who'll commission a perfume that only I will wear. The kind of man who'll sprinkle rose petals on our marriage bed." She sighed softly.

Tony rolled his eyes, knowing she couldn't see. "You made a face, didn't you?"

How could she tell? "Let's be realistic. When it comes to romance and marriage, a guy would like to wake up one morning, think let's do it today, grab his girlfriend and head for the nearest justice of the peace. No muss, no fuss."

"How horrible!" She glared at him. "You wouldn't even want your family there?"

"Families mess up everything," he said, thinking of Thea's wedding and the months of preparation—and the bills afterward. And for what? She and Peter still couldn't afford a place of their own. "When I was taping weddings, I saw more stressed-out couples. I saw brides hysterical because the rice bags were tinted the wrong shade of blue. And the whole time I taped, I never met a groom who didn't wish he'd eloped." Except Peter, who used the opportunity to read his poetry during the exchange of vows.

"An elopement could be romantic." But Alicia didn't sound convinced. "It would depend on how it was handled."

"I think a drive-through wedding chapel in Vegas sounds romantic." He smiled, anticipating her indignant response.

"Ick, but I've got to tell you, Georgia and I seriously thought about flying to Las Vegas and doing a whole show about wedding chapels. What do you think?"

"You just want a chance to talk the brides into something more elaborate."

"It's the grooms I want to talk to," she mumbled.

Tony laughed, something he found himself doing more and more often around her.

"Would you really want to elope?" she asked. "Is that the way you've always dreamed about getting married?"

"Ah...here again, men don't fantasize about their weddings."

"Think about it now."

All Tony could visualize was a blurry woman in white and a very tall cake. "I can't."

"Why not?"

"Because it would depend on the woman I'm marrying. But," he continued firmly, "the woman I marry will know I love her and she won't need perfume or flower petals or blue rice bags as proof. And she'd rather spend money on our future home than waste it on some overblown production where she's the producer, director and star."

Fortunately, the crew approached before Tony's and Alicia's disagreement could escalate. It was time to tape shots of Whitey, dressed in full armor, practicing riding a horse.

"You're just not a romantic, are you, Tony?" Alicia slid out from under his arm. "Here's your jacket back."

He missed her warmth. "You make it sound like a defect. I'd rather spend my money on something other than..." He searched for something frivolous and remembered the enormous rose bouquet his father had given his mother. "*Flowers*." He nearly spit out the word. "Flowers die, and then what have you got?"

Alicia was staring at him, her eyes enormous in her unsmiling face. "You have the memory."

"Will memories feed you when you're hungry?"

"Souls get hungry, too," she told him in a quiet voice. "I couldn't love a man who didn't believe that."

"You mean you'd prefer some guy who'd spend his last five bucks on a paperback of poetry rather than a rump roast?"

"Exactly!"

She'd just described his brother-in-law. Tony shook his head, deeply disappointed in her. "Fall in love with a guy like that if you insist, but for your sake, I hope you don't marry him."

The late-afternoon sun gilded the turrets of Camelot Castle. In the distance, Lake Travis glinted under a canopy of cloudless blue sky. Tony and his crew waited on the drawbridge, his back to all this picturesque glory.

How, Alicia asked herself, could anyone remain unmoved by such a sight? How could anyone tire of drinking it in? Was there truly no romance in the man's soul? Had he never felt romantic? He'd said his father was a musician; surely there'd been romance in his childhood. After their discussion yesterday, she thought she understood Tony better. She didn't agree with his outlook on life, but she did understand why they'd clashed so much in the past.

Alicia was intrigued, baffled and challenged all at the same time. Tony needed romance in his life. She might even do something about it.

But first, they had to tape the Camelot Castle segment. In spite of a lingering feeling of impending doom, Alicia had to admit that Whitey had planned a storybook proposal.

She picked up the radio microphone and pressed the transmit button. "Tony?"

"Yeah?"

From her vantage point inside the van, she could watch him as she spoke to him. "We're going to the gas station now."

"Okay." He waved. The sun gilded him, too, picking out copper glints in his dark brown hair. She sighed. In spite of their different outlooks on life, he was becoming more attractive to her each day.

She was going to have to try harder to resist the pull, since they could *never* be a couple. She shuddered at the thought. Live a life without romance? Never.

About half a mile from the restaurant at the highway interchange was a filling station where the car, driven by one of Amber's sorority sisters, would stop for some trumped-up reason. Alicia wasn't happy with this plan at all, but how else was Whitey supposed to come galloping up and sweep Amber away to Castle Camelot?

Unfortunately, the visuals at the gas station did not compare to the Southern plantation-style sorority house where Amber lived.

Jake drove around to the back of the station, where a nervous Whitey and two friends stood next to a horse trailer. As they watched, the horse's owner backed out a stunning white horse. Alicia caught her breath. "Look at the ribbons they've braided in the mane and tail," she said in an aside to Jake.

He mumbled something.

Honestly, were all men so unromantic? Would she ever find her soul mate? "Let's get some of this."

She approached a red-faced Whitey, who struggled to get on the rest of his armor.

"Man, this stuff is *heavy*."

"Let me get set up and then you can say that on camera. Hold the helmet in your arms." Alicia kicked cables out of the way and waited for Jake to set up the shot. It was just the two of them, since the sound tech was with Tony. The actual proposal would take place inside Castle Camelot.

Jake signaled her.

Alicia raised the mike. "While an unsuspecting—" she hoped "—Amber heads this way, Whitey and his white horse—" why hadn't she realized how stupid that sounded before now? "—get ready to sweep her away to Camelot." Alicia turned to Whitey. "You've been practicing for days." Probably hours, but who was counting? "Are you ready?"

"I guess so."

All the emotion of a codfish. "What does it feel like inside that suit of armor?"

Whitey shifted from foot to foot. "It's heavy, man."

Alicia had him hold up the helmet and asked several more questions. "Now this horse, Spun Sugar, has appeared in medieval reenactments, is that right?" Alicia had asked this question before, but for possible editing, she included it here. The owner answered some questions and then they watched as he decorated the horse, who looked more comfortable in his drapings than Whitey did. For a moment, Alicia was reminded of the old circus tiger and his ruff.

After she finished the interview, all they had to do was wait.

"Jake, is there any possible way to shoot so that the gas pumps aren't in the frame?" Alicia asked.

"Not without shooting toward the sun."

They both squinted toward the west where the sun was rapidly sinking.

"I wish Georgia was here," Alicia murmured, though she didn't know what Georgia could have thought of that she and Tony hadn't.

They'd hashed over alternatives last night. Even though Alicia couldn't find an acceptable alternative to the gas-station scenario, brainstorming with Tony hadn't been as difficult as she'd expected. They hadn't argued, either. There were times when she'd bitten her tongue and suspected that Tony had done the same, but all in all, the experience had been satisfying. She only wished they'd been able to magically transport Castle Camelot closer.

What was taking so long? Spun Sugar whinnied restlessly and shifted from side to side. Alicia checked her watch. "Whitey, does Amber usually run this late?"

Whitey, now in full armor, had propped himself against the station's compressed-air dispenser. "Yeah. She doesn't like to be the first one at a party."

Alicia sagged. At that instant, she heard the radio in the van. Running, she yanked open the door.

"Alicia?"

It was Tony. "What's up?"

"Amber just arrived."

"*What*?" she shrieked.

"She drove herself."

"And nobody told us?" Disaster. Alicia's mind raced. She'd known something would go wrong. She'd felt it.

"Tell me what you want me to do and I'll do it." Tony's voice was calm and sure. Dependable. Exactly the opposite of the way Alicia was feeling.

"Stall her until we get there." Frantically, she gestured to Jake, who came running.

"You got it."

Alicia told herself not to worry. Tony was experienced. He'd think of something. "Jake, pack up. Whitey, get on the horse and ride to the restaurant. Amber is already there."

Muttering unloverlike sentiments, Whitey struggled to mount the impatient horse.

"Don't forget your lance," Alicia called, then climbed into the back of the van.

After an eternity, Whitey galloped off. Alicia hoped he could see out of that helmet. After another eternity, Jake started the van. Alicia sat on the floor in the back, supporting the camera equipment and praying they wouldn't hit any bumps.

There was no way they'd be prepared to tape when Whitey came galloping up, even if they beat him to the restaurant, and there was some doubt about that. It was all up to Tony. He'd have to direct his cameraman and get both Amber's reaction and Whitey's entrance. He'd have to alert the restaurant's costumed waiters and waitresses that it was time to line up along the drawbridge.

Alicia closed her eyes. The success of this entire endeavor now rested with Tony. He'd said he'd been good. Now she'd see how good.

"Fifteen seconds," Jake called back to her.

Alicia prepared to leap out of the van. Jake swerved into the parking lot. Alicia opened the back of the van before it had completely stopped. "Just tape anything!" she yelled.

Whitey galloped past them, spraying gravel.

Alicia crawled out of the van to find that Tony, incredibly, had managed to get the "lords and ladies" outside to line the drawbridge. "Tape that!" She pointed to them and Jake hauled the bulky camera to his shoulder.

The drawbridge and the back of the horse was about all they could see from where they were in the parking lot. Alicia did direct Jake to try for some shots there, but she didn't think they'd be much good. He shook his head, indicating that Tony's man was in the way.

Alicia started running. Whitey leaned down and swept Amber up into the saddle with him, and the fabric of her dress billowed in the breeze. Amber was wearing a pale blue gown with silver trim, which suspiciously matched the ribbons on the horse, but it looked so great, Alicia forgave her. The crowd on the drawbridge cheered and threw rose petals at them as they galloped into the castle.

"Follow them inside!" Alicia started running. "I hope Whitey remembers to let us catch up before he takes her into the banquet hall."

Tony and his cameraman were ahead of them and Alicia didn't get the opportunity to ask if all had gone well.

Gasping for breath, she entered the cavernous foyer to see Tony getting a great shot of Whitey helping Amber off the horse.

Gesturing, Alicia signaled that she and Jake would head for the banquet hall. It wasn't what they'd originally planned, but that's the way it went sometimes.

Stepping into the great hall was like stepping back into another time. Silver, blue and white roping, banners and table runners decorated the hall. One long table spanned the length of the room, which had a huge fireplace at either end. On a raised dais, sat the visiting royalty, the soon-to-be-engaged couple's parents.

Alicia was so impressed she almost forgot to direct Jake.

"I'm setting up so I can get their faces," he said.

Tony would focus on the parents.

A murmur fluttered through the room. They'd been noticed. Alicia smiled and waved to everyone and put her finger to her lips, then moved it in a circle so Jake would start the camera.

Trumpets sounded, and Whitey, with Amber on one arm and his helmet on the other, clanked into the room. He led her to stand directly in front of her parents.

The fanfare died away.

Whitey cleared his throat. "My lord, my lady." He bowed to each in turn. "I, Lord Granger Alfred Whitfield II, have come to seek your permission to pay court to your daughter, the beautiful Lady Amber.''

Amber grinned. *At least try to act surprised*, Alicia grumbled to herself. Out of the corner of her eye, she saw Tony and his cameraman set up their shot. As soon as Tony nodded that they were taping, Alicia directed Jake to tighten the shot and concentrate on the couple.

After some more lord thising and lady thating, Amber's father pronounced, ''Lord Granger Alfred Whitfield II, I hereby grant you leave to address my daughter.''

Whitey removed his metal gloves, took Amber's hand and, with an awkward squeaking and clanking, got down on one knee. ''Amber,'' his voice cracked, ''my lady love, wilt thou be my wife?''

That quaver in his voice gave Alicia hope. Audiences went wild when the men choked up.

''Oh, Whitey, I can't believe you did all this.'' Amber giggled and looked all around. She waggled her fingers at her friends.

Edit, Alicia thought to herself.

''Amber? This hurts my knees.''

''Oh.'' She curtsied and giggled again. ''Yes, Lord Whitey, I'll marry you.''

A cheer rose from everyone except Alicia. Whitey struggled to his feet and waved. One of his fraternity brothers, dressed as a court page, came forward with a ring on a pillow. Even from a distance, Alicia could see it was quite a rock.

She thought of the tiny diamond chips in Lillie Patterson's ring and the love on Raul's face when he presented it to her. In contrast, Whitey looked smugly satisfied.

"Oh, Whitey, oh, Whitey!" With a little hop, Amber held out her hand and wiggled it. The ring was tied to the pillow and Whitey had a hard time getting it off.

"Hurry!" Amber urged him.

Alicia looked across the room and met Tony's eyes. He leaned over and said something to his cameraman, then made his way over to Alicia.

"How's that for emotion?" He indicated Amber, who was squealing and staring at her hand. Within seconds, she was surrounded by her chattering sorority sisters.

"Wrong emotion. That's greed." Alicia leaned against the stone wall. "She never once looked at Whitey. She didn't fling her arms around him or kiss him or anything. That is a woman who was engaged and waiting for her ring."

"Not everybody reacts the same way."

Alicia held out her arm and pushed up her jacket sleeve. "Look—no goose bumps." She blinked her eyes. "No tears."

Tony drew a long breath. "Yes, we did manage to get everything in the can. You're welcome."

She touched his arm. "I'm sorry. Yes, thanks. You bailed me out."

"Just doing my job."

But it wasn't his job. He'd done far more and she had yet to acknowledge it. "If I couldn't have had Georgia with me, I'm glad I had you. I know traveling on location has inconvenienced you and I haven't told you how much I appreciate your support."

Tony looked down at her and blinked his great dark eyes. Alicia thought he was pleased. She knew it when he smiled. "Thanks." His smile widened.

He hasn't been given many compliments in his life. Alicia didn't know where the thought came from, but she knew it was true. She thought about how she'd taken it for granted that he would get the shot. How in the past, she'd assumed he'd get funding or permission or market their show. He was dependable, quiet and good at what he did—the sort of personality it was easy to overlook. And she had.

"This—" he gestured to the scene before them "—will be okay. Tell you what. We'll get them to kiss and splice it in."

Alicia shook her head. "That would be lying."

"It would make better television. But no matter, this all looks great."

"Did you notice how her dress conveniently matches the decor?" Alicia nodded to the parents on the dais. "And why didn't her mother come down and hug her? I'll tell you why—because this is old news. They've already hugged over it."

"I choose to believe that Amber had her dress first and her friends secretly matched the decor to it," Tony said.

"And I thought you weren't a romantic," Alicia teased.

"And I thought you were," Tony shot back.

The trumpets sounded again and the restaurant's waiters and waitresses began the medieval pageant for which the restaurant was known.

Tony took her elbow. "Come on. Let's go outside where it's quieter."

With the sun gone, the air was chilly, and the twilight sky was clear and bright.

"Look at the moon!" Nearly full, it hung like a giant spotlight, turning the lake into a mirror. "Let me get Jake to tape—"

"Wait." Tony stayed her arm. "Let's enjoy the quiet first." He turned to lean against the rope railings of the bridge. Laughter, feminine squeals and ribald singing echoed from the banquet hall.

"Good idea." She joined him at the railing.

The huge moon looked as though it had silvered a path over Lake Travis. On the other side, the castle's shadow fell across the water and up the side of the cliff.

Alicia shivered.

Without asking if she was cold, Tony simply opened his jacket and drew her next to his chest. Alicia gladly accepted his warmth and leaned back against him. His arms crossed under hers and his chin rested on the top of her head. He seemed so matter-of-fact about sharing his coat that Alicia tried not read anything into the gesture.

But somehow, standing close in the moonlight seemed more intimate than sharing the jacket in broad daylight while sitting in the back of the equipment van. Alicia wondered if Tony felt the same. There was no way to ask him.

With the sound of his steady breathing in her ears, and his chest warm against her back, she was forced to acknowledge that her feelings toward him had undergone a profound change—and were changing still. She wasn't certain that was wise. They each had fundamental differences in their outlooks on life, differences that couldn't be resolved or compromised.

But for right now, Alicia enjoyed being held by a handsome man in the moonlight on a castle bridge. "This is romantic," she whispered. "And it doesn't cost anything." She turned her head to smile up at him and met his dark gaze.

The unexpected intensity of it held her captive. She was powerless to turn away. All at once, she became aware of the tension in his arms and the fact that only inches separated her mouth from his.

Neither moved. Alicia could see her thoughts mirrored on Tony's face. Both were aware that their relationship would be forever changed by closing the gap between them. Each weighed the consequences while trying to gauge the other's feelings.

"Alicia—" Tony's voice was quiet, yet deliberate "—I'm going to kiss you unless you stop me now."

"I wouldn't dream of stopping you," she whispered.

Alicia would never forget the possessively tender expression on Tony's face in the moments before he kissed her. Instead of instantly claiming what she'd granted him, he turned her gently in his arms until she was facing him. His hand crept to the back of her head, where he entwined his fingers in her curls and explored their texture. All the while, his gaze roamed her face as if memorizing each moonlit feature, at last meeting her eyes.

Alicia's lips tingled in anticipation. Her heart beat harder than it had when she'd raced to the castle.

And Tony spoke to her with his eyes. Eyes she'd previously found dark and inexpressive were a kaleidoscope of emotion. Curiosity, anticipation, pleasure, doubt and resolution—she sensed the feelings as clearly as if he'd spoken. She, who for years had found Tony Domenico closed and withdrawn, was astonished by the emotions she perceived within him.

She felt the pressure at the back of her head as he urged her closer and then his lips took hers.

Anticipating the feel of his mouth was one thing, the reality was another. At the touch of his lips, Alicia gasped. She couldn't help it. It was as though each nerve ending in her body had been concentrated in her lips. Tony immediately deepened the kiss.

Alicia's knees trembled and she drew her arms around his neck to keep from falling.

When at last he broke the kiss, Tony touched his lips to her forehead and held her trembling body close. "I'll never again look at the moon without thinking of you," he murmured with a kiss to her temple.

Snug in his arms, Alicia smiled. Tony was just as much a romantic as she was—he simply didn't know it yet.

CHAPTER SEVEN

MONDAY was a scheduled day off, and with everything proceeding so smoothly, Alicia sent the crew away on their own. She intended to talk with Georgia and explore Austin for future story ideas.

Now it was time to tell Tony her plans for the day and Alicia didn't know how to act. After last night's moonlight kiss, they'd rejoined the festivities and eaten dinner, then rehashed the whole Camelot Castle segment while they drove back to their motel. Since the crew pulled in right behind them, Tony had merely seen her to her door and said a quick good night.

She'd half expected him to call her after he'd reached his room and felt disappointed when he didn't, but it *had* been very late. So, now what? Did Tony consider their kiss a prelude to a personal relationship or merely a pleasant interlude in the moonlight? The fact that they were professional colleagues complicated everything.

Alicia stood in front of the bathroom mirror and practiced various approaches. "Hi, Tony!" Pleasantly breezy. Not bad. "Hi, Tony." Shyly sweet. Um, no. "Hi, Tony." A serious, where-do-we-go-from-here tone. Too much. "Hi." Cautious and do-you-feel-as-awkward-as-I-do? That one might be best.

It would help if she knew her own feelings. How *did* she consider that kiss in the moonlight? Fabulously magical. Who would have thought Tony could kiss like that?

Everything about the kiss was perfect. Exactly the way she would like to be kissed by the man she loved. But she didn't love Tony and he didn't love her. They couldn't. It was impossible. They were simply two people who'd collided while going in different life directions.

Therefore, she should practice "pleasantly breezy" until she could pull it off.

An excuse to see him would also help. She'd already walked across the street to buy breakfast at the all-night fast-food place—at five o'clock this morning because she couldn't sleep—so a breakfast invitation was out.

"Stop obsessing!" she ordered herself and took several deep breaths. She was making too much of the situation. "All right," she muttered, crossing the room. "I'll check on the Wichita Falls proposal and stop by Tony's room on my way out. If he offers to explore Austin with me, fine. If he claims he has work to do, fine."

Alicia found the number of the woman who would be in the third proposal and punched it.

"Rita? This is Alicia Hartson with 'Hartson Flowers'." Alicia smiled. People could hear the smile even though they couldn't see it.

"Oh, thanks for calling. I'm so sorry..."

Alicia's smile disappeared as she listened to the lone female proposer of her group. Rita had left a message at the studio yesterday, and no one had yet retrieved it.

"Saturday was my birthday and my boyfriend proposed!" Rita gushed.

Though sorry that the Valentine special wouldn't have a woman proposing to a man this year, Alicia was happy for her. Privately, she thought there was something sad about a woman having to propose.

After hearing the whole story, Alicia congratulated Rita, wished her well and hung up the phone. *Now* she had something to discuss with Tony. She wished it could be something else, but...

Grabbing the files with the names of the alternates, she locked her door, jogged down the corridor to Tony's room and rapped on the door while she still had the momentum.

"Come in," she heard. Didn't he know better than to leave his door unlocked?

She opened it to find him on the phone. When he saw her, he held up a hand, so she sat in the stuffed chair and waited.

He listened and scribbled, then froze and looked straight at her.

I know, she mouthed, guessing that he was listening to the studio messages and had just heard the one Rita had left.

"You heard about Wichita Falls?" he asked the instant he hung up the telephone.

Alicia nodded. "I called her this morning."

"I suppose this cancels our day off, which I was going to use to work anyway." With a grimace, he tossed his pen across the surface of the desk.

I was going to work anyway. Key words indicating that the kiss that Alicia had lost sleep over was in the pleasant-moonlight-interlude category.

A disappointment sharper than she'd anticipated ripped the layer of indifference in which she'd shrouded her feelings for Tony. But was this hurt pride she felt or something stronger? Whatever it was, she didn't want him to suspect anything.

"Yes, I'd planned to scout Austin for story ideas since it's one of our strong regional markets. Well, these things happen." Breezily professional. Alicia was proud of herself.

She unzipped her portfolio. "Now here are the three alternates..."

"Hartson Flowers" was probably the biggest thing ever to hit Roperville, Texas, Alicia thought as she waited for Jake's nod.

They were at the town marina, where Tony was checking on permits and Alicia was taping her stand-up introduction.

Jake signaled.

"We're here in east Texas for our third proposal." She grimaced. "Sorry. We don't know in what order they'll be shown. I'll start again."

She stood, faced the camera, collected herself, then smiled.

"We're here in the beautiful east Texas town of Roperville, known for some of the best lake fishing in the state. Behind me is Lake Roper, where our prospective groom, Trey Baker, wants to propose to Debbie Silsby by spelling out 'Will you marry me?' using sailboats."

Alicia went on to give a little background about the couple, then told Jake to cut. "I'm freezing!" She eyed the dark sky and the angry lake with whitecaps whipped up by the wind. "We should redo that intro when the weather improves." She had to raise her voice to be heard over the wind.

Hurrying to the shelter of the marina, Alicia ran into Tony on his way out.

"All set?" she asked.

"Yes." He squinted at the sky, but didn't say anything. He didn't have to.

"Let's go to the hotel. We've been at this for hours and I'm starving." She ran for the car.

"And you're cold, too. Why don't you ever wear a coat?" Tony opened the car door for her.

"Because it doesn't look good on camera." Alicia scrambled inside and wrapped her arms around herself.

Tony closed the door, but stopped to talk with the crew before joining her in the car. "We're not staying at the same place. The hotel was full, but I found a bed and breakfast where we can stay."

"Any place where I can get a cup of tea and take a hot bath is fine with me." She rubbed her arms.

He grinned. Alicia smiled back at him, then transferred her gaze out the window.

They'd worked for hours yesterday setting up the new third proposal. They'd driven all the next day and had arrived in Roperville in the late afternoon. They'd worked cooperatively, efficiently and very, very professionally together.

The kiss might never have happened.

Alicia tried to tell herself that was what she wanted, but had to admit she was miffed. Maybe more than miffed. Was kissing her so unmemorable? Wasn't Tony affected at all? And...would he ever kiss her again?

Tony knew there was going to be trouble as soon as he saw Charlotte's Inn. The huge Victorian gingerbread house sat on a private road overlooking the lake.

The place screamed romantic weekend getaway.

And he'd booked the crew at a downscale roadside motel with cable TV.

He and Alicia would be alone here.

She'd think he'd set this love nest up on purpose. And if the crew saw it, rumors would be swirling around the studio by the time they returned next week.

The crisis yesterday had been a divine gift designed to knock sense into him. Kissing her had been completely inappropriate, no matter how appealing she'd looked or how much he'd wanted to or how right kissing her had felt.

Alicia Hartson was a business associate. She was a friendly, open person and he'd taken advantage of the situation. He'd been prepared to apologize and he was grateful that she'd apparently chalked up his aberrant behavior to a bit of moonlight madness to be forgotten in the light of day.

It was humbling to realize that she could easily dismiss something that had affected him so profoundly, but he knew it was for the best.

And now this. He wouldn't blame her if she slapped his face.

Wondering whether to explain that the crew had opted for cable TV and the men were all going to have to share one room anyway, Tony slid a look toward Alicia. She stared at Charlotte's Inn with her lips parted and her eyes all starry.

"Tony." His name was a hushed whisper. "It's beautiful." She turned to look at him. "How did you ever find this place?"

Mentally kicking himself, he met her gaze. "It does look great, doesn't it?" He forced himself to smile and hoped she'd realize he'd had no idea what the place looked like when he'd booked the rooms. "Just the sort of place where you can have your tea." *And I can get an old-fashioned belt of whiskey.*

He parked the car and they walked inside, with Alicia oohing and aahing every step of the way.

"Oh, good, you're just in time for tea." An elegantly dressed, gray-haired woman met them in the foyer and led them into a parlor, where a silver tea service sat on a low table by the fire. Windows on either side looked out onto the lake. Storm clouds had darkened the afternoon. A misty rain had begun to fall.

While Tony stared out the windows in dismay, Alicia headed for the tea table. Behind him, he could hear her greeting the three other inhabitants of the room.

"Tony, may I pour you some tea?" She smiled up at him, her face eager and open.

He tried to match her smile. "Later. I'm going to carry in the luggage before the rain gets heavier."

A tiny sigh escaped as Alicia watched Tony leave the room. She couldn't believe Tony—*Tony*—had booked them into this charming bed and breakfast. How had he found it?

And the fact that he was embarrassed by his gesture made her heart turn over. He *was* a romantic after all. She sipped her tea, feeling a warmth she knew wasn't due entirely to the hot liquid. Tony *thought* he didn't believe in romance because he'd never been in love. And now he was.

Tony was in love with her.

The explanation was so simple, Alicia couldn't believe she hadn't realized it before. Hadn't she always believed love would strike like a lightning bolt? That's what had happened to him. There was no way a man could kiss a woman the way Tony had kissed her without being completely and totally in love. The whole kiss had been an homage to love.

She sighed again, and idly selected one of the tea cakes to eat. This place was so romantic and he was being so awkwardly sweet.

But of course he felt awkward. He didn't know how *she* felt yet! And she felt...charmed. Alicia was honest enough to acknowledge that she wasn't in love with Tony yet.

But she was well on her way.

Every hotel and motel room in the entire town was spoken for. There was a marching band and flag corps competition going on in a nearby city and Roperville was getting the overflow. Tony quickly realized he'd been lucky to find rooms at all. Charlotte's Inn was expensive and Tony had hoped to use that as an excuse for moving them if he could, but now he and Alicia were stuck here for at least one night. More, if the weather didn't improve. Judging from Alicia's expression when she saw the place, he'd never pry her away. The best he could hope for was a sunny day tomorrow, so they could tape.

Feeling damp and cold and thinking the fire in the parlor looked really good, Tony signed the guest register. Only one of the rooms had an en suite bath, which he surrendered to Alicia.

"Will you and your party be having dinner with us this evening?" asked the woman who'd welcomed them earlier.

"Yes," Tony answered. Not getting out in this weather appealed to him.

She smiled conspiratorially. "I'll put you two young people in the alcove. We serve aperitifs at six. Dinner at seven."

Tony checked his watch. Nearly four-thirty. "That'll be fine."

It was not fine.

Alicia's room was on the ground floor, and Tony's was on the third, so he'd agreed to meet her in the parlor.

He saw at once that he was underdressed. Three other couples, all of retirement age, chatted with her in the parlor. The men were in jackets and the women wore dresses. Tony had changed into cotton khaki pants and a burgundy shirt, but had not brought anything dressier with him. Fancy dinners weren't in the schedule or in the budget.

Alicia wore a black suit and some sparkly earrings. She looked great, but she always looked great.

Tony stood in the doorway and watched her charm the other guests—the way she'd charmed him. A room took on a different personality when Alicia Hartson was in it. Vibrant and effervescent, that was Alicia, and people became more animated just being around her. Her partner, Georgia, was just as much a people person, but in a quieter more intimate way. People confided in Georgia. People tried to please Alicia.

Tony shook his head. The two women were good together, and Alicia wasn't doing such a bad job on her own, either. He definitely should take them to the networks after this show.

"Tony, there you are!" She crossed the room to meet him, took his hand and literally pulled him into the parlor.

Privately amused, he allowed himself to be drawn into a discussion about the history of Charlotte's Inn, thinking how easily Alicia worked with people. She linked her arm with his, which surprised him, but he didn't object.

Moments later, their hostess informed them dinner was ready and, with a smile, led Tony and Alicia away from the others to a small round room off the parlor. "This is Lovers' Alcove," she announced with a sly smile and disappeared.

Tony actually felt his blood run cold.

"Oh, Tony!" Alicia breathed with a look that couldn't have been softer if it had been filmed through gauze.

"I thought we could discuss tomorrow's schedule in privacy here." That excuse probably sounded as lame to Alicia as it did to him. "And if the weather doesn't improve, our third couple can use this as a setting for their proposal."

If anything, the expression on her face grew softer. She touched his hand and sighed. "It's okay. You don't have to justify reserving this room. You thought I would enjoy it." She sat back and smiled. A tender, intimate smile. "That's reason enough."

His mouth dry, Tony reached for his water goblet. Fate had set events in motion and there was nothing he could do. And honestly, he didn't know what he wanted to do.

Alicia leaned forward, chin propped on her knuckles. Tony eyed her warily over the rim of the goblet.

"I want to know all about Anthony Domenico."

Tony gave a self-deprecating laugh as he set the goblet down, watching to see that he didn't knock it over. "There's nothing much to tell."

"Oh, I think there is." She sipped her water, her eyes never leaving his.

Tony's breathing quickened. Forces he didn't understand were at work here. Powerful forces he shouldn't attempt to thwart. Across the tiny table was a beautiful woman who had given him her complete attention. A beautiful woman he'd held in his arms not so many nights ago. A beautiful woman he'd like to kiss again and again until his head spun.

The beautiful woman spoke. "Tell me about your family. You have nieces?"

Tony inhaled and, with the light, sweet scent he'd forever associate with Alicia filling his lungs, began to speak.

Once Tony began to speak, he couldn't seem to stop. It was as though she'd only known a black-and-white version of Tony and now he was in full, living color.

Alicia listened, half in wonder, half in sympathy, to stories about his parents and sister and his brother-in-law, Peter the poet.

Tony recounted the stories with a gentle exasperation that told Alicia he worried about his family constantly. She began to understand some of the responsibility he'd assumed at an age when most people were still wondering what to do with their lives.

He also revealed far more about himself than he realized. Alicia had had years of interviewing experience. She was fairly good at filling in the gaps people left when they talked to her, and Tony's gaps revealed a man who'd had to grow up too fast and in the process had become somber and serious.

By the time the chef had brought bowls of thick gumbo, Tony had Alicia intrigued. During a crisp green salad, intrigue turned into admiration. Admiration became a genuine liking and a desire for friendship during the main course—Tony had beef, Alicia grilled chicken—but it was just prior to dessert when she fell in love with him.

She knew the instant it happened, the instant when fondness no longer described her feelings for Tony and love did.

His torrent of words had slowed to a trickle. He reached across the table and took both her hands in his. "I needed to talk about my family." He looked at her hands as he spoke. "I don't know how you knew, but thanks for listening." Then he lifted her hands and kissed her knuckles—not a mere grazing with his lips, but a genuine heartfelt kiss.

Alicia stared at his bent head with its thick dark hair and then into his eyes when he raised them to hers.

He smiled, his expression so honest and open she felt the purity of it pierce her heart.

That's when she fell in love.

She should have expected it. Since the moment he'd kissed her in the moonlight, she'd been teetering on the brink. But Tony's revealing himself to her pushed Alicia over the edge.

He released her hands when the owner of Charlotte's Inn appeared in the alcove to inquire about dessert. In a complete fog, Alicia agreed to something she had no idea she was agreeing to.

Tony Domenico. Handsome, honest, yet never drawing attention to himself. The man who had supported her for years, whether she'd realized it or not. A man who revealed a depth of character she'd never even suspected.

The man she loved.

Okay, so it wasn't a lightning bolt the first time she saw him. Once she started to fall for him, she fell hard and fast. She had the goose bumps to prove it, too.

When the gray-haired woman brought dessert, it turned out to be an artfully arranged platter of cookies, fruit and chocolates. After pouring coffee, the woman set the pot on the table and withdrew, saying, "I won't bother you two anymore this evening."

Alicia stared at the platter without really seeing it. She was still recovering from the realization that she'd fallen in love when she hadn't expected to.

A newly silent Tony plucked the largest, reddest strawberry, dipped it into a tiny pot of chocolate and held it out to Alicia. She was forced to open her mouth and catch a drop of chocolate before it dripped onto the white tablecloth.

Tony laughed softly, his expression now tinged with a darker emotion. ''I want to know all about Alicia Hartson,'' he echoed her earlier words. ''Tell me about your family.''

The strawberry turned bitter in her mouth. She swallowed, telling herself that his question was innocent and well-meaning. He couldn't know that she refused to discuss her family.

She started to tell him as much, then hesitated. This very private man had just poured his heart out to her. She believed that she was in love with him and suspected he felt the same way about her. She couldn't refuse to discuss what passed for her family.

For a moment, he thought she wasn't going to answer.

''My father died when I was eight.'' She took a butter cookie and avoided meeting his eyes. ''My mother remarried when I was ten, and my stepfather and I didn't get along.''

The flat, colorless voice didn't sound like hers. ''I'm sorry.'' He said it automatically and wished he'd thought of something different to say.

She made a tiny gesture of dismissal and toyed with the cookie, eventually reducing it to a pile of crumbs. ''I wasn't his daughter. I was an extra expense. He . . . complained about every cent he spent on me. Mother kept telling me we had to be grateful we had a roof over our heads.'' She brushed the crumbs from her fingers but still didn't look at him.

"I left home as soon as I could." Now she met his eyes. "It's hard for me to talk about this."

His heart went out to her. "Then you don't—"

"Yes, I do." Her chin tilted in that determined way she had.

Wordlessly, Tony reached for her hand. It felt cold in his.

"I thought...I thought that with me gone, Mom could leave him."

"And she didn't."

Alicia shook her head.

"I think I met your mother and stepfather when they toured the studio." His voice was neutral, but he remembered the man asking how much money Tony paid his daughter. Not stepdaughter—daughter. Tony hadn't told him and there had been several unpleasant moments as a result. Tony tried to visualize Alicia's mother and only remembered a quiet, unassuming, featureless person. Unmemorable.

"When Mom didn't leave him, I realized it was because she didn't have any place to go, so I rented a two-bedroom apartment as soon as I could afford it and told her she could come live with me. But she stayed with him."

Hearing the little-girl hurt in her voice, Tony gently squeezed her hands. "Perhaps she didn't want to be a burden to you."

"The way I was to her?"

Her expression was raw and vulnerable, a wounded child asking for reassurance.

"You would never be a burden to anyone," he said firmly. "Your mother must love your stepfather. That's why she stayed."

"How could anyone love *him*?"

And not me, was what she didn't say. "Well, I met him and..." Tony was about to say that the man wasn't so bad, but stopped. He stared into her hurt blue eyes. "And I don't know. The man's a toad."

Alicia blinked, then a surprised laugh bubbled out of her. Her fingers flew to her mouth as if to hold the laughter back.

"I shouldn't have said that," Tony apologized. But he wasn't sorry.

Alicia dropped her hand and a wide smile stretched across her face. "Yes, you should have. He *is* a toad." She laughed again. "I've spent years trying to win the approval of a *toad*!" She continued to laugh until tears glistened. Dabbing at the corners of her eyes, she went on, "And I still live in a two-bedroom apartment, just waiting for the day my mother realizes she's married to a toad instead of a prince."

With a rueful shake of her head, Alicia drew a deep breath and visibly collected herself. She gestured to the dessert platter. "Look at all these pretty goodies and we've barely touched them."

Tony watched as she exclaimed over the chocolates and tried to figure out which one might have coconut in it because she said she loathed coconut. The old Alicia was back, but now Tony knew that lurking inside was a little girl who just wanted to be loved.

CHAPTER EIGHT

"Oh, Alicia, I'm glad I caught you!"

"Georgia, what's the matter? Are you okay?" Clutching the telephone, Alicia sat in the window seat of her bedroom and braced herself for bad news.

"I'm fine, but I just got this letter from a man in Odessa. He wants his proposal to be on our show."

"Next year, I hope."

"No, right now. It's better than the boats—have you taped the boats yet?"

Alicia looked out onto a gray and rainy landscape. "It's still raining. We haven't done diddly-squat."

"Then tell the guy you're sorry the weather didn't cooperate—he's an alternate anyway, right?—and get to Odessa."

Alicia drew her legs up and rested her head on her knees. She was reluctant to leave this little bit of heaven. The fireplace, the quiet . . . Tony.

In spite of their romantic dinner, he was obviously waiting until they returned to Houston before openly admitting his feelings. Abandoning this proposal for another would hurry things along and Alicia was all for that.

"Tell me what's so great about the Odessa proposal," she asked Georgia.

"The man..." There was the sound of rustling paper. "Philip. Philip wants to propose in a hot-air balloon."

"We've done that."

"*But* he's planted a field of white pansies spelling out 'Marry me, Sue?' and he'll fly the balloon over. He sent a picture and he's really done it. Isn't that romantic? Won't it look great?"

Alicia closed her eyes as goose bumps rose on her arms. A good sign. She hadn't had goose bumps since the circus. Or since she'd sat across from Tony at dinner the other night. She sighed. "You're right. I'll talk to Tony about it. Fill me in on the particulars."

Georgia did and then they chatted a few minutes about how the twins were growing and Georgia's stomach was growing and how she despaired of ever again squeezing into a size six. After hanging up the telephone, Alicia stared out the window and wondered why she hadn't told Georgia of her new feelings for Tony. She'd always thought that when she fell in love, she'd want to shout it to the world, but now she found herself wanting to savor the feelings alone. Tony's caution was rubbing off on her, she thought ruefully.

Well, now she had a perfectly valid excuse to seek him out. She found him working at a table in the parlor. "I thought you'd be in your room."

"The maid's cleaning it," he answered with a smile.

Alicia took a good, hard look at that smile. It was warmer than mere courtesy, but it was definitely restrained. It was a "wait" sort of smile. Okay then, she'd wait. After all, she'd waited all her life to find her true love; another few days wouldn't change her feelings. "I just talked with Georgia."

Immediately all business, Tony flipped to a clean page on the lined pad in front of him. "What's up?"

Yes, they were unquestionably in a holding pattern. Alicia pulled a chair over to the table. "See what you think of this."

"Hi!" Alicia, wearing her red blazer, smiled into the camera. "The 'Hartson Flowers' team is standing on the plains of west Texas where Philip Pressman is going to propose to Susie Vancamp...."

Tony leaned against the van and watched Alicia work. She'd surprised him, astonished him, actually. Just when he'd been afraid that he'd lost her to the insistently romantic atmosphere of Charlotte's Inn, she'd suggested they fly to Odessa to tape this proposal rather than wait on the weather in Roperville to clear.

He would have expected her to make the most of her time at the inn. Frankly, he'd anticipated some awkward moments, but once again, Alicia proved that she was a professional and his admiration for her increased.

Since the drive from Roperville in east Texas to Odessa in west Texas took eleven hours, he and Alicia had chosen to fly. The van set out with their equipment early on Friday. Tony and Alicia had driven to the nearest airport and had taken a morning flight. By the time the van arrived, they'd met with Philip and had planned the entire segment.

Today, Saturday, they were taping background. A cold front was due to move through the area, bringing winds, but clearing skies. Tomorrow morning, they planned to tape the actual proposal.

Tony hoped all went well. If so, he could be back in his office on Wednesday. Tuesday, if they pushed it.

"Tony? What do you think? Should I tape an intro from over there?" Alicia pointed to the field behind her.

Tony shook his head. "You don't need it. If there's time, you might try one tomorrow when the balloons are out."

"Good idea." Alicia approached, holding out her hand for her clipboard. "Let's see . . . Jake and I'll be in the second balloon. Do you want a chance to go up with Philip and Susie?"

"I'm not going up," Jake said from behind her. "I don't like heights."

"Then you'll get ground shots," Alicia responded, completely unruffled. "Tony, you and your cameraman will go up in the second balloon and I'll take a camcorder and go up with Philip and Susie. I'll tell them I'm making a souvenir video of their flight. I can do the voice-over later." She scribbled as she spoke.

Tony knew she'd just rearranged all the assignments without missing a beat. She'd put together this entire segment with a proficiency he admired and she'd just as quickly changed it—all so her cameraman wouldn't have to go up in a balloon. She didn't argue, didn't try to change his mind. She just dealt with it.

The perfect blending of practicality and romance.

Tony's mouth went dry. Staring at her bent head, he fought a sudden desire to touch her. The urge was so overwhelming that he had to step to the other side of the van so he couldn't see her. Once there, he leaned against the side, turning his back to the heart logo. Staring out across the winter-brown field, Tony acknowledged that his feelings for Alicia Hartson were stronger than a friendly working relationship would accommodate. He'd probably always felt that way, though he'd tried to convince himself that he didn't like her, that she irritated him and that she was too impractical.

But she wasn't impractical and she'd proved it several times on this trip alone. Look at how readily she'd abandoned that paradise-for-romantics, Charlotte's Inn. She'd enjoyed herself while she was there, but when it was time to leave, she left, and didn't look back.

Tony was the one who'd been looking back. He remembered their dinner and the way Alicia had looked. He remembered her face as she'd told him about her loveless childhood. *He* was the one who'd fallen under the spell of Charlotte's Inn.

But it didn't matter how he felt about Alicia or if she felt anything for him. After the Valentine special, she and her show would be heading for either New York or Los Angeles while he stayed in Houston. That's the way it had to be. He didn't have the right to hold her back—assuming he could. And once she was back home and immersed in her routine, she'd soon forget him.

The best Tony could hope for was to remain a fond memory.

*   *   *

"What a glorious morning!" Wearing her light-weight red blazer, Alicia shivered and looked at the clear, bright blue sky. On the ground, two balloons were being inflated and the huge fans hummed in the background.

Philip paced nervously and checked his watch over and over. "I told her I'd won this balloon flight in a contest," he said. "She didn't seem too excited about it."

He'd already told Alicia that several times, but she pretended he hadn't. "She'll be here." Alicia patted his arm.

"I don't know." He shook his head. "She doesn't like to miss church."

Alicia glanced over at Tony to see if he'd heard that. He, his cameraman and the sound tech were checking the equipment, which they planned to load in the second balloon by the time Susie arrived so she wouldn't see anything and get suspicious. Jake had covered the "Hartson Flowers" logo with the white magnetic signs they used to conceal their identity when necessary.

"You've got the ring, haven't you?" Alicia asked, though she knew he did.

Philip patted the breast pocket of his jacket and looked at his watch again. "I'm going to go call her." Abruptly, he turned and headed into the small trailer the balloon agency used as its office.

Philip was one nervous groom-to-be. Usually the men had settled down by now and only got nervous while actually proposing. Alicia chalked it up to the hurried arrangements they'd made.

Everything was ready and she took a few moments to watch Tony. The hotel where they were staying was a clean, modest and perfectly adequate facility without a shred of character or charm. Alicia swallowed a sigh over the loss of Charlotte's Inn. Ever since they'd left, Tony had submerged his romantic streak. Honestly, she understood—or thought she did—but he could be a wee bit friendlier without the crew suspecting anything.

"Alicia!" He called to her, then jogged over. "You're going to freeze up there."

"It's cold," she admitted, "but I'll be okay."

"It'll get a lot colder with the wind." He shrugged out of his leather jacket. "You're taping. If you shake, so will the camcorder." He draped his jacket around her shoulders and took the tiny camera from her. "Wear my jacket."

"But what will you wear?" The fleece lining felt soft against her cheek. It was almost like having Tony next to her. She quit protesting, pushed her arms through and zipped the jacket.

"The balloon company has windbreakers. I'll grab a couple of those."

"But I could wear—"

"They wouldn't be warm enough for you." He touched his fingers to her cheek. "And I want you to be warm."

Alicia felt his touch all the way to her toes, but it was the tender expression on his face that warmed her heart. He *did* care. Feeling as buoyant as the balloons, Alicia stood on her tiptoes and kissed him on his cheek. "Thanks, Tony," she said.

He looked surprised by her action but pleased, too.

"I see her car! I see her car!" Philip pointed, then ran over to them. "She actually showed up!"

He gulped air. "She really came! What'll I do now?"

Tony's cameraman had loaded the equipment, so he headed for the second balloon. Alicia gave Philip last-minute instructions. She'd already told him everything before, but her voice seemed to calm him. "Try not to be so nervous. Remember, I'll be right there!" With a push, she sent him off to greet Susie.

Susie towered over Philip. Susie towered over nearly every man in the vicinity. This was going to be an interesting visual.

Snuggling into Tony's jacket, Alicia deliberately stayed in the background. After introducing herself as the videographer, she stayed out of the way. She didn't *think* Susie would recognize her, but didn't want to take any chances.

The fans filling the balloons made too much noise for Alicia to tape anything while she was standing near Philip and Susie. She hoped that Jake, back at the van, was taping for background footage. Ideally, either she or Tony would be directing and watching from the monitors in the van, but Jake was experienced enough to make some decisions on his own.

Alicia lagged behind and taped as Philip and Susie climbed into the basket. Susie had accepted her presence without question, for which Alicia was grateful.

Alicia had been up in a balloon before, but from Susie's white-knuckled grip on the ropes and murmured comments to Philip, Alicia guessed it was her first ascent.

The balloon pilot turned up the burner, and with a sound that always made Alicia think of a dragon's breath, the basket rocked, then rose gently and easily. The earth fell away. As they began to drift, Alicia began to watch for the white pansies Philip had planted. Would Susie be able to read them? Would the balloon go in that direction?

Tony's balloon was launched after theirs but quickly matched them in altitude.

"It's so quiet up here. I expected wind and noise," Susie said.

"Yeah." Philip was nearly paralyzed with nervousness.

Alicia longed to reassure him but was wary of spoiling the surprise.

"Are we going to have a picnic somewhere?" Susie asked and indicated the cooler under the corner bench.

"I dunno," Philip mumbled.

"Well, didn't you ask?" Susie persisted.

Philip shook his head.

"I think that's the champagne." Alicia couldn't stay quiet any longer. Poor Philip looked like he was about to fling himself over the side of the basket.

"Champagne?" Disapproval sounded in Susie's voice. "I don't drink."

"I didn't—"

Alicia interrupted him. "Champagne is a tradition after a balloon flight. I believe there is also sparkling cider."

Susie looked only slightly mollified. Philip looked miserable.

"Smile!" Alicia started videotaping. Behind her, she could hear the roar as Tony's balloon fired its burner. Other than that noise and their own, there was an unearthly peace and quiet. There was no sensation of moving; it seemed more as if they were still and the earth was moving under them.

The balloon pilot caught her attention and she lowered the camera. "Coming up on the right," he said.

Alicia zoomed in with the telephoto lens and saw a white tracing far below them. "Can you get lower? I can barely make it out. Better hurry."

Poor choice of words. However, after a descent that left her stomach queasy and Philip green, Alicia could easily read the pansies. She nodded to Philip, waved to Tony, braced herself against the side of the basket and proceeded to tape.

"Uh, Susie?" Philip tapped her on the shoulder.

Susie was gazing in the opposite direction from the rapidly approaching field of pansies.

"Look at the view!"

"Uh, there's an even better one over on this side."

Stop saying "uh", Alicia mentally directed him.

"Is there?" Susie walked to the other side.

Philip lunged to insinuate himself between Susie and the view.

"Philip, you're in the way. I can't see."

"Susie." He took hold of both her arms. "I love you."

"That's nice, but I can't—"

Alicia's stifled chuckle jiggled the camera.

"Susie, I love you *a lot*." Determination filled his voice.

"Philip?" Susie darted a look at the pilot and Alicia. "Philip, we aren't alone."

"I don't care. I want the whole world to know how much I love you." He drew a deep breath. "I love Susie Vancamp!" he shouted.

Way to go, Alicia silently cheered. She made a mental note to ask him about that shout during the wrap-up interview. "Philip, what's gotten into you?"

He stepped aside so Susie could look over the edge of the balloon basket. "*That's* what's gotten into me."

Susie squinted. "There's writing. It says—"

Philip broke in. "It says, 'Will you marry me, Susie?'"

"It says, 'Marry me, Sue?'" she corrected.

Was there ever a more oblivious bride-to-be?

"Okay, I ran out of pansies," Philip said with understandable irritation.

"You mean *you* did that?"

Alicia captured Susie's stunned look. Perfect. She felt the goose bumps forming.

"Yes."

There was silence. Too much silence. A suspenseful silence. Alicia's goose bumps flattened.

"I can't believe you did that," Susie said.

"Well, I did!"

"Why?"

"Because I love you and I want to marry you!"

If Philip didn't shake that woman, Alicia was afraid she would.

"But nobody calls me Sue," Susie said.

"I..." Helplessly, Philip looked at Alicia.

Balancing the camera with one hand, she patted her chest.

Philip reached into his pocket and withdrew a navy blue ring box. Opening it, he cleared his voice. "Susie Vancamp, will you marry me?"

Gasping, Susie clasped both hands over her mouth. "You *did* plant those pansies!"

The words were muffled. Alicia would let the sound tech fiddle with the mix. Or maybe they could cut in one of Tony's shots. He *was* getting this, she assumed. She wished she could look, but that would ruin her own tape.

Philip hadn't dropped to one knee, but in this case, it was fine. If he'd done so, Alicia wouldn't have been able to back up far enough to get them both in the frame.

Anyway, her goose bumps were back. Susie's vocal utterances had been reduced to "Oh, Philip" and "I can't believe you did this" or variations of the same.

She had not answered his proposal.

Philip, too, had been waiting for the all-important yes. "Susie?" He took the ring out of the box.

"Oh, I . . ." Susie looked at the camera and at the balloon operator, then back to a tense Philip. Her hands dropped from her mouth. "Yes, Philip," she said and held out her hand.

His hands shook as he placed the ring on her finger. Alicia zoomed in, but her eyes were tearing and it was difficult to see through the viewfinder. She managed to keep taping while Susie allowed Philip a chaste kiss, then turned off the camera and congratulated them.

Grabbing the two-way radio, she called Tony. "Did you get it, did you get it?"

She could see him laugh and bring the microphone up to his face. "Yes, I did. I can tell you're crying. How about the goose bumps?"

Alicia grinned and made a thumbs-up. "Say, can you zoom in on me? This'll make some great parting footage, don't you think?"

She took off Tony's jacket and stood and waved, then gestured to the panorama spread out beneath them.

They'd done it. They'd taped the three proposals. Thinking about it, Alicia thought they'd probably run them in the order they'd taped. The faked emotions and overly staged medieval-knight-on-horseback segment bothered her, but Tony was right. It *would* make good television. Waving at the other balloon, she saluted him and shrugged back into his jacket.

By Tuesday, they'd be back in Houston. But first they had to return to Roperville and get their car. Tomorrow morning, the crew could take off directly for Houston. As for Tony and Alicia, as soon as they got back to the motel this afternoon, she intended to make reservations for them at a certain romantic Victorian bed and breakfast.

Lost in her own romantic fantasies, Alicia didn't pay much attention to Philip and Susie.

The jeep chasing the balloons radioed them about a field where they had permission to land. Alicia intended to visit the pansies with both Susie and Philip and there was the wrap-up interview before she could truly call this Valentine special complete.

The wrap-up wouldn't take long. Alicia could tell that Philip and Susie were private people and Susie was uncomfortable in their presence. Wait until Philip told her his proposal was to be featured on "Hartson Flowers".

The balloon set down with hardly a bump, and Alicia clambered out with the bottle of champagne and two glasses, leaving the cider for Susie and Philip.

"Tony!" She watched his balloon settle on the ground and the sphere collapse. "Open this!" She handed him the bottle.

"Hey, I saw you running with it. It'll explode."

She laughed. "I have every confidence that you can master something as insignificant as a champagne cork."

"Somebody's in a good mood," he said. Kneeling, he took off his windbreaker and used it as a pad to keep the cork from flying off.

"Of *course* I'm in a good mood. It was great! The balloon flight, the proposal—"

A muffled thud signaled that Tony had opened the bottle. In spite of his precautions, champagne hissed and a wet spot dampened the jacket.

"Oops," Alicia said.

"If I had to get anything on my souvenir jacket, I'm glad it was champagne." Tony filled the glasses and handed her one. Standing, he asked, "Other than a safe landing, what do you want to drink to?"

There were many things she could have said, Alicia supposed, but having just seen yet another woman achieve romantic bliss, Alicia was bolder than she might ordinarily have been. Deliberately, she touched her glass to Tony's. "Let's drink to us."

Then she waited. She'd made the first move, but he was going to have to take the first sip.

"Are we drinking to a successful partnership?" There was a husky note in his voice.

"We could."

"Alicia..." Longing uncertainty washed over his face, then faded away. "Then let's do it right." Leaning down, he kissed her lightly, in front of the crew, the balloonists and anybody who cared to look. "To *us*," he said, and raised his glass.

CHAPTER NINE

ALICIA was happily stunned. Kissing her in the field was the most romantic gesture Tony had ever made. Even more romantic than booking Charlotte's Inn.

She wanted to melt against him, she wanted to jump up and down and throw her arms around him, she wanted to shout, but she knew such an exuberant demonstration would make him uncomfortable. In fact, she was surprised he'd so openly kissed her. Knowing how much the romantic extras meant to her, he'd overcome his natural inclination for private, no-frills romance and was allowing his romantic nature to bloom. The gesture touched Alicia beyond words, so she, too, made an effort at compromise and kept her reaction low-key, trying to communicate her feelings with her eyes.

It was probably just as well because, within moments, the crew approached for instructions and Alicia had to confer with Philip and Susie. She sipped at her champagne once more before reluctantly handing the glass to Tony. "Later," she whispered and thought his eyes warmed in response. Then she picked her way over clumps of dried grass to the newly engaged couple. "Philip, did you tell her the news?"

"There's more?" Susie raised her eyebrows.

Alicia didn't need to see Philip's uneasy look to know he hadn't told Susie about appearing on TV.

"You bet there's more!" Alicia shifted into her television mode. "I'm Alicia Hartson with 'Hartson Flowers'. You've heard of our show?"

"Yes . . ." She didn't sound too certain.

Alicia went on, "Then you'll know that each year, we feature surprise marriage proposals on our Valentine special. And congratulations, Susie. Philip's proposal to you is going to be featured on this year's special!"

The color drained from Susie's face. Not a good sign.

"Don't worry," Alicia reassured her, "you looked great. It'll be very moving."

"You mean you're not the souvenir-video person?"

Alicia shook her head. "But don't worry, we'll see that you get a copy of the show. Right now, though, we'd like to go to the field where Philip planted the pansies and tape some shots of you two."

"Okay." Philip slipped his arm around Susie's waist. Susie stiffly tolerated his touch.

Alicia tried to ignore Susie's restrained mood. *She's just overwhelmed. It'll be all right*, she told herself and signaled Tony that they were ready to go to the field.

Alicia was exhausted, but exhilarated, by the time they made it back to the motel. The three crewmen took off to have dinner and sample the Odessa nightlife and Alicia looked forward to time alone with Tony.

Tony. Sighing, Alicia whirled around and collapsed on her bed. Tony. *Tony*. She hugged the pillow to her chest. She could hardly wait to see him, to talk—

The phone rang. Tony couldn't wait, either. Smiling to herself, Alicia stretched across the bed and answered the phone with a sultry "Hello."

"Miss Hartson?" The uncertain voice was *not* Tony's.

"Yes?"

"This is Susie Vancamp. I—I've got to talk with you."

"Susie!" Alicia bolted upright. "What is it?"

"I can't…I don't know what to do!" she wailed.

Alicia calmed her down and arranged to meet her at a nearby pancake house. Then she called Tony.

"Alicia." His voice was a warm caress.

Unfortunately, Alicia couldn't enjoy it. "We might have a problem. Susie just called me and she's very upset."

"Upset about being featured on the program or upset about marrying Philip?"

Alicia closed her eyes. "I don't know. I'm meeting her in half an hour. Stand by and I'll let you know what's happening."

"Do you want me to come with you?" he offered.

"No." But Alicia was glad he'd asked. "I think she'll do better one on one."

Susie was already waiting for Alicia when she arrived ten minutes early. The woman looked distressed but not hysterical.

Alicia slid into the booth. "Would you like something to drink?"

"No," Susie said, then changed her mind. "Iced tea, please," she said to the hovering waitress.

Alicia ordered the same, though she had a feeling she'd want something stronger. "You seemed upset when you called," she began.

Susie exhaled. "This whole day has been..." She gestured wordlessly.

"Wonderful?" Alicia supplied with a hopeful smile.

"Astonishing. I didn't know Philip was going to propose."

"Good. Our viewers love surprise proposals."

"Well, I don't."

Her forceful statement pretty much squashed any hope Alicia had of a happy outcome to this meeting.

"Philip and I have never even talked of marriage. I've been aware for some time that his feelings for me were stronger than mine for him. I thought he knew that." She shifted uncomfortably, waiting until her tea had been set in front of her before continuing. "The fact is, I don't know how I feel about him. Marriage is a big step, and he isn't the sort of husband I'd imagined for myself."

"Sometimes love catches you by surprise," Alicia said softly, thinking of Tony.

"I'm not sure that I *do* love him," Susie said. "That's the problem."

"I saw your face when you agreed to marry Philip—remember, I was taping the whole thing. I think you love him." Alicia didn't want to go into her goose bump theory. Neither did she want to convince this woman that her feelings weren't important.

"You saw his face, too. He had his wounded-puppy look on." Susie slammed her glass down. "I *hate* being manipulated, and that's what he did. How was I supposed to turn him down or ask for time or...or anything! There we were and there you were and the way he was looking at me all hopeful and pathetic—ahh!" She grimaced and buried her head in her hands. "If I'd turned him down, he would have flung himself over the side of the balloon."

Alicia regarded her and thought back to those moments in the balloon. "I don't think that's the only reason you accepted." Pointedly, she glanced down at Susie's left hand, where Philip's engagement ring twinkled.

Following her gaze, Susie self-consciously covered the ring with her other hand. "Well, he *is* sweet and I do like him and he went to all that trouble, but..."

"You felt pressured by the situation."

Susie nodded. "The thing is, I'm just not sure, and feeling that way, I shouldn't have signed that release paper for your show. If I give Philip back his ring and then everybody sees what happened, it'll be horrible."

So don't give Philip back his ring. Alicia held her breath.

"*Please* don't put Philip's proposal on your show. He should never..." Susie's eyes teared. "He *knows* I hate the name Sue!" She sniffed and grabbed for her iced tea.

Alicia's heart sank. She would, of course, honor Susie's request, but didn't want the young woman making any hasty decisions. She started to tell her so when Susie began talking. It quickly became obvious that she needed to talk to someone, and Alicia was that someone.

"You have to understand that Philip never thinks things through. He wants to please me, but he never gets it quite right. Look at the pansies." Her face softened. "He knew they'd survive the cold weather, so that's why he chose them. But he ran out."

"And you know he was thinking about you the whole time he was planting them," Alicia pointed out, taking heart from Susie's expression. Alicia thought she knew how Susie felt. Susie had fallen in love with a man she never expected to and wasn't quite ready to relinquish the mental image she'd carried with her since girlhood.

In fact, Alicia knew *exactly* how Susie felt because she felt the same way. She'd thought Tony was too much like her stepfather, a miser with a dictatorial streak. But Tony had compromised— more than compromised.

And Alicia loved him for it.

"I know Philip went to a lot of trouble." Susie sighed. "But..."

Alicia reached across the table and squeezed Susie's hand. "I don't want you to feel in any way obligated by 'Hartson Flowers'. This is a decision that will affect the rest of your life. Take all the time you need." She reached into her purse for a business card and scribbled Georgia's number on the reverse. "We'll be in postproduction by Friday. If you decide to let us feature your proposal, then call this number and Georgia will find us. I can't make any promises that we'll work it in, though.

We need a third proposal, so we'll be taping an alternate.''

Susie took the card. "I'm sorry I caused all this trouble.''

"Don't apologize." Alicia finished the last of her iced tea. "Your happiness is more important than a television show.''

Tony stared across the tiny Formica table in his room. "I can't believe you told her that her happiness is more important than your Valentine special!''

"Well, it is!" Alicia glared at him with a defiant tilt to her chin.

"Of course it is!" Tony exhaled heavily. "I just can't believe you told her that.''

"Why? Did you think—" Alicia broke off with a shake of her head. "You thought I'd be so overwhelmed by Philip's proposal that I'd tell Susie to overlook her reservations about Philip, the man? That hurts my feelings, Tony.''

"No, I didn't mean that." But hadn't the thought crossed his mind? Alicia had gone on and on about the pansies, and Tony had to agree that when they were standing in the middle of them all, the sight of hundreds of white pansies with their dark purple centers had been very impressive.

Tony found himself unexpectedly resentful. Alicia was terribly impressed by a bunch of flowers and a ride in a hot-air balloon. And how about the guy who put on a suit of armor and rented a horse? Big deal. The circus was a bigger deal, but still nothing that great.

Amateurs. These men were all amateurs. Now, if he were planning a splashy proposal, the entire world would get wet. His proposal to Alicia would become legend in the annals of surprise proposals. Alicia would be telling the story forever. Their children would grow up on it. Their grandchildren would—

Alicia. Was he thinking of proposing to Alicia?

His heart picked up speed. Sometime, somewhere, the woman seated across from him—now studiously avoiding his eyes as she shuffled papers—had gotten under his skin. Now he was thinking of a future with her. He couldn't imagine a future *without* her.

But what about the future waiting for her and Georgia? Alicia was just the sort of romantic who would turn down an opportunity at the networks so she could stay in Houston and be near him. Tony couldn't let her make that sacrifice. No, he had to be noble.

Searching for a way to lighten the mood, he took a pencil and drew a star, then handed it to her.

"What's this for?"

"It's a gold star. I'm trying to tell you I'm proud of you, Alicia. Suffering financially, but proud."

She regarded him for a moment, then grinned. "Oh, you're not doing too badly. Look." Turning papers to face him, she pointed. "We'll go back to Roperville and tape the sailboats. The crew can have time off after we get back to Houston, so that'll save hotel and travel expenses. I can even salvage some balloon footage for a segment on another show. I'll change the voice-over and no one will ever know it was originally scheduled for the Valentine special."

"You're amazing," he said softly.

"So I've been told." Smiling, Alicia leaned forward and rested her chin on her hand. "But not nearly often enough."

"Perhaps I can do something about that," Tony said, leaning forward to kiss her.

Nobility, he discovered, was highly overrated.

To Alicia's dismay, Charlotte's Inn was full. In fact, everything within twenty miles of Roperville had been booked because of the Southwest Regional Marching Band and Flag Corps Competition. Obviously, this was worthy of a "Hartson Flowers" segment—if Alicia could wangle it. But their first priority was finishing the Valentine special.

The weather, though clear and cold, was windy, with rain predicted for later in the week. The van was still en route from Odessa and would arrive late tonight. Tuesday was the first day they would be able to tape. They were racing both the clock and the weather. A quick phone call to Georgia revealed that Susie had not contacted her, so it looked as though Trey Baker's sailboat proposal would have to be the one.

Alicia and Tony split up to finalize arrangements and would meet over a late lunch to discuss the details.

"What would you think of running the special with just two proposals?" Tony asked as they sat down in the hotel restaurant.

"Isn't it a little early to call it quits? We've already done the preliminary work. I know the weather is iffy, but we'll know by tomorrow if the taping's a go."

He nodded and ran his hand through his hair, unaccustomed weariness in the gesture.

Alicia took in his somber expression and the new shadows under his eyes. "You're worried about something and it's not the show. What's wrong?"

Tony shook his head as if refusing to answer her question. Alicia speared a piece of lettuce from her salad and waited. She hoped he'd confide in her but knew better than to push.

"I need to get back to Houston," Tony said at last. "It looks like my brother-in-law, the poet, is bound for Europe."

"And you want to say goodbye."

"No," Tony corrected, "I want to say good riddance." His jaw hardened. "Peter's leaving because he says he needs solitude to create. He submitted some of his poems to a literary publication. They were rejected."

"I'm sorry."

"Rejection is not new to Peter. But according to my sister, it was felt that Peter's poetry was shallow."

"Oh, dear."

"Actually, I feel vindicated." He smiled without mirth. "His poems never did anything for me. However, when such a comment comes from a respected literary publisher, Peter takes notice. Therefore, he 'feels the need to replenish his well of creativity with new experiences.' And apparently, only an extended stay in Europe—away from his wife and three children—will suffice."

Tony's fingers closed around his fork. Alicia thought it was a very good thing that Peter was in Houston and Tony was in Roperville.

"And how does your sister feel about this?" She imagined Tony's sister must have been very upset to put such dark circles under her brother's eyes.

"Oh, Thea's all for it. And so are my parents. In fact—" Tony slapped his hands on the table "—they want to sell their stock in my company and give it to Peter to pay for the trip!" Disbelief and frustration sounded in his voice.

Alicia frowned. "I didn't know Domenico Cable sold stock."

"It doesn't."

His words were clipped and Alicia thought he might regret confiding in her.

"My parents are financial innocents. So is Peter. So is my sister." Tony pushed his food away, untouched. "When I was financing the studio, Pop insisted on 'helping'. And I let him because I thought that when my parents spent all their money, at least they'd have this little bit left. So I took his money and told them I'd invested it. That's when I made up the stock story. I've been paying them quarterly dividends ever since. That's what they've been living on."

No wonder he'd always been so money conscious. Alicia knew he'd plowed most of his profits back into the shows he syndicated and equipment for the studio. And besides himself, he was supporting his entire family. "Oh, Tony." She wanted to hug him. If they hadn't been sitting in a restaurant, she might have. She settled for reaching across the table and grasping his arm.

He covered her hand with his. "It's not your problem. And the thing is, my parents look on it as helping Peter achieve his dream the way they helped me achieve mine. What am I supposed to say? No, I won't sell the stock?"

Withdrawing her hand, Alicia shook her head. "What if you give them however much Peter needs and tell your parents you didn't have to sell all the stock. That way you can still give them some money."

He considered her suggestion. "That's a good idea. I might try it. Unfortunately, my assets aren't very liquid at the moment. I need to do some shuffling."

Alicia knew he'd recently invested a lot in the Valentine special. No wonder he wanted to cut the trip short.

Tony's hand curled into a fist. "I can't stand the thought of Peter blowing my parents' life savings on a self-indulgent trip to Europe when he's still living with his in-laws because he can't support his own family!"

"Maybe you can talk to your sister about it."

"Thea?" Tony rolled his eyes. "She thinks anything Peter does is wonderful. She's nuts."

He sounded so disgusted that Alicia couldn't help smiling. "She's supporting the man she loves."

Tony looked straight at her. "Is that what love does to people? Blinds them to common sense?"

"Not unless they were blind to begin with." Alicia tried to tell herself he was talking only about his sister, but she suspected he wasn't. "Peter's going to Europe right now doesn't make sense to you, but people do a lot of things that don't make sense to other people. They're just following dreams."

"Why am I always the one who pays for other people's dreams?" It was a question straight from his heart.

She smiled. "Because that's the kind of man you are."

Tony stared at his plate. "What if I'm tired of being that kind of man?"

Then he could change, but Alicia knew he wouldn't. "You know, part of this is your fault."

"*My* fault?"

"Yes. You've been supporting your family, letting them think they had money, and now you're upset because they want to spend what they believe is theirs."

"Of course I'm *upset*. What do they think they're going to live on?"

"Well, maybe Peter will become a huge success."

He stared at her, an expression of distaste on his face. "You're just like them, aren't you?"

"No, I—"

"Of course you are. I remember our discussion. You said the man of your dreams would spend his last five dollars on poetry and not rump roast." He crumpled his napkin and stood.

"I was speaking hypothetically." Only now did Alicia fully understand the weight Tony had given her words—and why. "If I were hungry, I would certainly prefer the rump roast." She looked at him from under her lashes. "But maybe it could be a smaller rump roast so there would be money left for a bottle of red wine to go with it?"

"It would have to be really cheap wine." A reluctant smile tugged at the corners of Tony's mouth.

Alicia was glad to see that smile. "Sit back down and eat." She pointed to his chair. Tony sat and Alicia pushed his plate in front of him. "Relax. I've decided that this Valentine special will be so successful and you'll make so much money selling it, that you could send not only Peter, but your entire family to Europe with him."

Picking up his fork, Tony reminded her, "There was the question of solitude."

"Ah, yes. And it was solitude at a great distance, was it not?" Alicia raised her eyebrows.

Tony nodded.

"Support is one thing," she said. "But letting your husband roam around Europe while you live in your parents' home and chase three kids is something else. Now that I think about it, Tony, your sister *is* nuts."

He put his palm over his heart and bowed. "Thank you."

"You're quite welcome," she replied.

And they both laughed.

During the rest of their lunch, Alicia set about cheering Tony up. She told him all the most amusing stories from her "Hartson Flowers" adventures.

He laughed and she liked making him laugh. His eyes lit up and creased at the corners but didn't leave lines. Such skin was wasted on a man, she thought. Best of all, he finished his lunch, a sign that he was no longer brooding about his flighty family.

When they walked back to their rooms, he casually dropped his arm around her shoulders. She tried her best to read something romantic in the gesture but couldn't.

She was losing him, she thought. He was turning into a friend. Not that having Tony Domenico for a friend was bad, but Alicia wanted more.

Their rooms were across the hall from each other. They stopped in front of her door and Alicia tried to figure out a reason to invite Tony in—surely there was some paperwork about something that needed his attention or approval?

His arm slid from around her shoulders and he caught her hand. "Alicia, thanks. I know you were trying to make me feel better and, well, you did." Smiling, he leaned forward and dropped a chaste kiss on her temple.

Something snapped inside Alicia. She would *not* let him get away with another unsatisfying kiss. They weren't in a field and there wasn't a table between them. There was no reason at all for her not to melt against the man she loved.

So when Tony tried to let go of her hand, she gripped it, then placed it at her waist while she drew her other arm around his neck.

"Alicia?"

"Close your eyes and think of moonlight."

His eyes drifted shut. "And what are you thinking of?"

"This." Standing on her tiptoes, she kissed him.

For the briefest instant, Alicia sensed a struggle going on inside Tony. Then his arms tightened around her as he lifted her off the floor.

CHAPTER TEN

HE SHOULDN'T be kissing her this way, but he couldn't seem to stop.

The instant Alicia's lips touched his, Tony knew he was lost, along with all his good intentions. He was selfish—he admitted it. He wanted Alicia to spend her life with him. It was all he could do to keep from blurting out, "Let's get married," and eloping with her to Vegas or Reno.

But that's not the way Alicia would want it. She wanted a grand proposal, and abandoning his noble intentions, he decided to see that she got one.

With a surge of happiness fueling his muscles, he lifted her above him. She weighed hardly more than his nieces. How could someone so light and fragile be his strength? She anchored him and gave him flight at the same time.

Alicia, with her practical streak, would become the bridge from his parents' world to his. She would teach him to fly and become *his* safety net.

He loved her and longed to tell her so.

But not here, in the dingy hallway of a moderately priced tourist-class hotel. Knowing Alicia, she would store the moment when he told her he loved her with her keepsake memories and he wanted the time and place to be special for her. Worthy of her.

Slowly, he lowered her to the ground, memorizing the feel of her body against his, the shape of her mouth and the way she tasted.

"Tony, I—"

"Shh." He put a finger to her lips. "Wait."

"Tony." She was all misty-eyed determination.

And he was equally determined. Silently, he held out his hand for her card key.

Exhaling heavily, Alicia muttered, "I'll do it myself." Jamming the card into the lock, she opened the door, then turned. "Tony—"

He was already across the hall at his door. "Call me when you've contacted Trey's sailing buddies, okay?" Lifting a hand in farewell, he closed the door behind him and leaned against it. He'd been too abrupt in parting but hadn't trusted himself another instant in her presence.

For the first time, he understood why people agreed to let their proposals be filmed. They wanted to share their joy with the entire world. Alicia felt the same way. It didn't matter than he didn't. What mattered was that he wanted to please her with the grandest proposal she'd ever seen.

Now all he had to do was figure out how.

Wait? Wait for what? And for how long?

Frustrated, Alicia paced across her small room. Surely he'd guessed she'd been about to tell him she loved him. And he'd stopped her. Why?

Did that mean he didn't love her? Or that he did? Did he want to say it first? Then why didn't he? Was he concerned about the impropriety of developing a personal relationship while on business?

She *wanted* to be improper, darn it all. Sighing, she stared at the closed door. She should march right across the hall, bang on Tony's door and shout that she loved him, regardless of who could hear.

Or was he still afraid she was like his family? He was such a private person. Alicia knew it cost him a lot to confide in her. He'd been angry with his brother-in-law and rightly so. Feeding your soul was one thing. But feeding your family was more important and it appeared that Tony had been carrying that responsibility for such a long time that *his* soul was starved.

Banquet time, she decided, smiling to herself.

Alicia stopped pacing as a thought struck her. Tony must be concerned that she'd object to his supporting his family. Either that, or he didn't want to ask her, or any woman for that matter, to share the burden with him.

The silly man. They could work it out. They could work anything out and she wanted to tell him so.

Wait, he'd said. Alicia didn't want to wait. And she wasn't going to.

Tony leaned back in the uncomfortable armchair and covered his eyes. They were gritty from lack of sleep and the hours he'd spent bathed in the light from the exposed bulb in the hanging lamp over the worktable in his hotel room.

But he had a plan. It involved calling in a few favors and incurring a few debts, but it was well worth the trouble.

He'd arranged press credentials for "Hartson Flowers" at the Regional Marching Band and Flag Corps Competition. College bands from a five-state area were competing for the right to attend the national competition later in the spring. They'd honed their shows during the preceding football season and were at their peak form. Alicia would cover the competition—knowing her, she could get an entire half-hour show out of it—and during a break in performances, Tony planned to propose— with the help of a stadium full of people.

He'd set up breakfast meetings with stadium officials and a choreographer. He'd found a printer and his proposal was set for Thursday. Alicia would be surprised, stunned and, he hoped, very, very happy. She'd cry. She'd turn into one giant goose bump.

And she'd say yes.

Massaging the aching muscles in his neck, he flipped off the light and stretched out on the bed for a couple of hours sleep. He had a real flair for this stuff, he thought as he dozed off.

"Was I wearing the pale pink or the bright pink jacket when we filmed the intro here last week?" Alicia asked Jake as they stood on the pier.

"Bright pink," he said.

She'd have to take his word for it since she honestly couldn't remember. Alicia returned to the van and changed from her pale pink jacket to the bright pink one.

She checked her appearance in the side mirror and touched up her blush. Too pale. One might even suspect she was nervous, because she was. Today, she was going to tell Tony she loved him whether or not he wanted to hear it.

And then she was going to ask him to marry her.

During the long, sleepless hours of the previous night, Alicia had decided that by proposing to Tony, she could allay any lingering fears he had that she expected "every day to be Valentine's Day." Just a simple question that required a simple answer. No muss, no fuss, just the way he wanted it.

He'd left her a message with the hotel operator that he was checking details for the shoot. What details, he didn't say. Alicia had ridden to the marina in the equipment van.

While she, in the wrong-colored jacket, was interviewing Trey earlier, she'd noticed Tony drive up and disappear into the boat-chartering office. Business as usual. Entirely proper, yet disappointing.

"Alicia!" There he was now, waving to her from the doorway.

She slammed the door to the van and trotted over to him. "What's up?" Scanning his face, she hoped for a glimmer of a smile or a softly spoken greeting.

Nothing. They might have been strangers. "The manager expects a marine warning to be posted within the hour. We've got to get those boats out on the lake or we'll lose another day." Tony cast a worried look at the approaching line of clouds.

Alicia put her personal feelings aside and concentrated on the problem at hand. "Have you told Trey?"

"I radioed him from the office." Tony pointed across the lake where Trey and his sailing buddies were readying the five sailboats. "They're working as fast as they can."

Alicia nodded. "How does he plan to explain our being on the boat with him?"

Tony's face was blank. "On the boat with him?"

"Well, yes. How else are we to film Debbie's acceptance?"

"I—I hadn't thought about it." Drawing his hands to his waist, he stared across the lake.

Alicia refrained from pointing out that it had been his responsibility to go over this detail with Trey. Tony was fraying a bit around the edges and obviously hadn't slept much, if at all. Alicia would cut him some slack. Especially today. *Especially* today. "Don't worry." She touched his arm to give him support and because she needed to touch him just then. "I'll think of something. Maybe we won't have to go with him at all. Jake can shoot telephoto and we can hook Trey up with a wireless mike. How about that?"

"Sounds okay," Tony said absently.

Alicia gave him a fondly exasperated smile that he didn't see.

"Hey, you TV folk!" called the man from the charter office. "The wind has picked up. Nothing's going to be allowed out of the marina in a bit. Can't have the boats bumping into each other." He lowered the all-clear flag that flew above the building and raised the one warning of a weather change.

Tony's breath hissed between his teeth.

"Tony, look, it's only Tuesday. We still have the rest of the week."

"That's cutting it close," he said.

He wanted to return to Houston, she could tell. "Why don't you contact Trey and let's see what we can salvage today? I'm sure he's as impatient as we are."

Tony nodded, but he didn't look at all optimistic.

Alicia stared after him, then transferred her gaze to the boats across the lake. The pier provided a perfect view of them, and it gave her an idea. Turning to look behind her, she spotted a line of covered boat slips.

"Jake!" She beckoned for him to follow her and they walked down the weathered wooden boards to the slips. "Do you think you could tape from here and still get a shot of those boats across the lake?"

He shrugged. "Let's see."

When he was in place with the camera, Alicia walked back to the end of the pier. Of course, Jake and his huge professional camera stuck out like a sore thumb to her, but she wasn't an unsuspecting Debbie Silsby. If Trey stood at the end of the pier with Debbie, and the boats unfurled their sails with the signs, the proposal would work without the boats ever leaving their moorings.

Now if Trey would only agree.

Trey, having postponed his proposal once before, was ready and eager to "get the whole thing over with."

Alicia reviewed the revised plan with Trey, Tony and the crew. Tony set up his cameraman in the marina office. Alicia stayed with Jake.

Then they waited.

Alicia could hardly bear the waiting. Never before could she remember being so impatient to finish a segment. She toyed with the idea of asking Jake to tape her proposal to Tony, but knew it would embarrass both men.

No muss, no fuss. That's what Tony'd said he wanted. Alicia wouldn't have minded a little fuss, but that could happen afterward. She imagined Tony shouting, "Yes!" and picking her up and twirling her around the way he had in the hotel hallway. She—

"Here they come." Jake pulled the camera and tripod behind an equipment locker in case Debbie looked their way as they drove in.

Alicia ducked behind the locker, too, since her bright pink jacket might attract attention. *Remember to turn on your microphone*, she mentally telegraphed Trey.

Trey parked his pickup truck. Debbie emerged, an outdoorsy-looking woman dressed in jeans and a windbreaker. Holding hands, the two young people slowly walked toward the pier.

Turn on the microphone.

Alicia looked at the sound tech, his hands pressing the earphones close. He shook his head.

Trey and Debbie were halfway down the pier.

Alicia grabbed the radio. "Tony! Trey hasn't turned on his mike."

"I'll take care of it." Within seconds, Tony casually walked outside the marina office, his hands shoved in his pockets. He'd donned the attitude of a man who was checking the weather.

It worked. Trey looked at Tony and froze. Alicia could see Debbie question him and Trey say something in response.

Tony waved and tugged on his ear. Trey responded with a jerky wave of his own.

"We've got audio," the sound tech said a few seconds later.

Alicia stepped from behind the lockers and waved once at Tony, then she sat next to the technician and grabbed another set of headphones.

"...was that?" she heard Debbie ask.

"Some guy I met here earlier." A rustling sounded as Trey's clothes brushed against the microphone. "Listen, Deb, I'm sorry we can't go out on the lake today."

"Me, too, but I'd rather do maintenance on a day like today than waste good sailing time," she said. Alicia liked her immediately.

"Deb." More rustling. Alicia could see that Trey had taken her hands. Good. He'd remembered to move closer. The audio would improve. "I've always loved sailing."

"I *know*." She chuckled. "You bought a boat before you bought your truck."

"Yeah. Anyway, I know how lucky I am to have found someone who loves to sail as much as I do, someone who can put up with my spending so much time on the *Trinket*." He chuckled softly. "But, Deb, I want you to know that as much as I love that boat, I love you more."

"Trey?" The quiver in Debbie's voice sounded clearly through the headphones. Goose bumps rose on Alicia's arms and legs. With a grin that spoke of long experience, the sound tech handed her a tissue.

"I . . ." Clearing his throat, Trey tried again. "In fact, if I lost you, I don't think I'd ever want to sail again."

"Oh, Trey." Debbie threw her arms around him. "You're not going to lose me."

I don't think I'd ever want to sail again was the signal for Tony to cue Trey's friends.

Across the lake, sails were raised and Alicia held out her hand for a second tissue.

"That's what I want to make sure of. So Deb...Deb..." Trey unlatched her arms from around his neck and gently turned her so she would see the sailboats across the lake.

"WILL YOU MARRY ME, DEB?" billowed and flapped in the rising wind.

"*Trey*!" she screamed and covered her mouth with her hands.

Alicia winced through her tears and the sound tech swiftly adjusted dials.

"Trey!" Debbie stared at him, her mouth open. "Is that for me?" She pointed.

In answer, Trey pulled out the ring box and opened it for her to see.

"*Yes*!" Debbie flung herself at Trey. "Yes, yes, yes, yes, yes!" She laughed and cried at the same time.

Alicia sobbed audibly.

"Shh," the sound tech cautioned.

"Watch it, you're going to push me in the lake!" Trey said, laughing, but he clutched her so tightly that if he went in the lake, it was certain Debbie would, too.

Wiping her eyes, Alicia signaled for Jake to stay put. Stepping outside the boat shed, she radioed Tony. "Tony, can your cameraman meet me on the pier?"

"Will do."

"Aren't you going to ask if that was a good one?"

"Are you kidding? There's not a dry eye in the house here."

Alicia laughed. Just wait until *she* proposed to *him*!

She probably rushed the wrap-up interview but didn't care. Soon Trey and Debbie were driving around the lake to tell the other sailors their good news.

The crew was packing up their equipment and Tony was thanking the charter-office manager for the use of his building when Alicia approached. Her knees were shaking. She hoped he didn't notice.

"Congratulations," he said, then bent to kiss her cheek. "You did it. This will be your best Valentine special ever. And if you tape some trailers, I'll express mail them to every first- and second-tier market in the country."

"Thanks, Tony."

He peered at her. "That's going to cost a fortune and all I get is a 'Thanks, Tony'?"

"Well, it's because I have something on my mind." She took his hand.

"That reminds me," he went on, "I made arrangements for you to tape at the band and flag corps competition on Thursday. The crew can have tomorrow off and we can tape on Thursday morning. We drive to Houston in the afternoon and you can start postproduction on Friday. How does that sound?"

"I thought you were in a hurry to get back to Houston." *She* was in a hurry to get back to Houston.

"This is an opportunity for you and I would never hold you back." His eyes were solemn. "The competition is a major event in these parts."

That was an odd way to put it, but Alicia didn't dwell on Tony's word choice. "I'm sure it is, but—"

"You should be there."

He looked so serious. Maybe he had a thing for marching bands. "Well, okay."

"Good." He released her hand.

Alicia would have preferred he hadn't, but that wasn't important now. What was important was her proposal. "Before the band competition, you should know that there's one more proposal."

"There's nothing on the schedule." He looked stunned. "You've got three—four if we use the balloon one."

"Tony...in the hallway yesterday, you interrupted me."

Comprehension dawned. "Alicia," he whispered, "don't."

She ignored him. "I wanted to tell you that...that..."

The look on his face stopped her. His mouth tight, his eyes darted from side to side as though he sought a way to escape. A trapped look.

That was not the emotion Alicia had wanted or expected to see. A coldness formed deep within her and raced through her veins, chilling her fingers and making her shiver. "I wanted to tell you...that I've enjoyed working with you these past weeks."

His face relaxed and he exhaled. "I've enjoyed working with you, too." Relief made his smile far too wide.

Her heart nearly stopped beating. He didn't want her to tell him how she felt. He didn't want her love. He must not love her.

He didn't love her.

Alicia could barely force herself to meet his eyes. "So I *propose...*" she began with deliberate emphasis.

His smile shrank and wariness crept back into his eyes.

Though her heart froze, Alicia forced herself to continue, "that we take our crew out and celebrate tonight."

"Great idea!" Tony actually clapped her on the shoulder. "I'll tell the guys."

Chilled from the inside out, Alicia stared after him. Whether or not Tony suspected she'd been about to say something else, she'd been spared the humiliation of actually speaking the words.

And this, she thought, rubbing her arms, *is what is meant by cold comfort*.

Tony spent the rest of the afternoon working out stadium logistics while Alicia conferred with Georgia on the proposals.

He almost thought he'd been mistaken in thinking she was about to confess her feelings for him, except for her bright and brittle performance at their celebration dinner.

She was hurt and he hated the fact that he'd hurt her.

And from now until he saw her at the stadium, they'd each be forced to pretend. He'd pretend that he didn't know what she'd been going to say, and she'd pretend she hadn't been going to say it. It would be best if each stayed out of the other's way.

Tony called her room on Wednesday morning, but there was no answer. With relief, he left a message at the front desk to tell her he'd be out the whole day.

By Wednesday night, Tony was running on pure adrenaline. How these other men could stand to include the stress of a production crew in their proposal was beyond him. He knew production, yet *he* found it stressful.

Tomorrow morning, he'd have to tell the crew what he planned to do. Though it would never be broadcast—he had to draw the line somewhere—Alicia would have her proposal captured on tape.

Tony grinned as he called her room Wednesday night. He wouldn't mind seeing the proposal a few more times himself.

"Hello?" A man's voice answered.

Tony was so shocked he let several seconds tick by.

"Hello?" the man repeated.

"I'm looking for Alicia Hartson."

"Sorry, you've dialed the wrong room." Click.

Shaking his head, Tony punched in the number more carefully this time. He'd be glad when they were officially engaged and his nerves were settled.

"Hello?" It was the same man.

"Sorry," Tony apologized and cradled the receiver. Blinking, he called the front desk. "Alicia Hartson's room, please."

"I'm sorry, Ms. Hartson has checked out."

Tony stopped breathing. "When?"

"This morning, sir."

Through dry lips, Tony managed to ask, "Did she leave a message for Anthony Domenico?"

"One moment."

It was the longest moment of his life.

"Mr. Domenico?" At Tony's assent, the clerk continued, "There's an envelope here for you."

Tony wanted to ask the clerk to read it aloud but murmured that he was on his way down. And Tony ran, arriving breathless and not caring what anyone thought. Ripping open the envelope, he read,

Tony,

I interviewed competition personnel and some of the kids today. All the segment lacks is footage that you can get tomorrow. I'm going to take a couple of days off. I'll finish postproduction on the Valentine special this weekend.

Alicia

"Did Ms. Hartson receive the messages I left her?"

The clerk returned the pink slips to him. Tony thanked her, thrust the slips into his pocket and returned to his room.

Alicia hadn't said where she was going. Tony called Georgia, who hadn't heard from her. He called the studio, he called her apartment and he called Charlotte's Inn.

No Alicia.

She was gone and he didn't know where she was.

CHAPTER ELEVEN

"You're in love with him, aren't you?"

"Who?" Alicia handed Georgia a pint of Death by Chocolate ice cream and a spoon. Then she sat next to her partner's bed and opened a pint for herself.

"Tony." Georgia delicately pried off the cardboard lid.

"I don't know why you'd think that." By the time Georgia got her lid off, Alicia had already consumed two mouthfuls of chocolate comfort.

"Possibly because it's eight o'clock in the morning and we're eating ice cream—ice cream with fat *and* sugar in it. The only reason to eat fat and sugar is man trouble. And the only man you've been around lately is Tony."

"Please." Alicia swallowed. "I have a three-man production crew."

"And not a one of them worth the calories." Georgia took her first bite and sighed. "Except Jake, if he'd cut his hair and shave."

"Hmm, Jake. He's quiet, obedient and doesn't speak until spoken to. The perfect man." Alicia dug at a chocolate chunk. "I'll have to give him serious consideration."

Georgia licked her spoon. "He called here."

"Jake?"

"*Tony*." Georgia looked at her. "He sounded concerned. *Very* concerned."

Alicia lifted a shoulder. "I don't know why. I left him a note." She ate more ice cream and grimaced as a pain shot through the side of her head. "Brain freeze," she said.

"Exactly what I was thinking. What happened?"

Alicia had known all along she would confide in Georgia and she promptly did, telling her the whole story up to and including the almost-proposal. Then she cried. By the time she finished, her ice cream was soft. *Good. Easier to eat*, she thought with a sniff.

Leveling a stern look at Alicia, Georgia balanced her own ice cream on her stomach. "Let me get this straight. You left Tony on location alone?"

"He can handle it."

"Excuse me, but taping segments for 'Hartson Flowers' is not *his* responsibility."

"Oh, come on, Georgia. This was all his idea. I've got the Valentine special to edit." Alicia tilted her carton, drank melted ice cream, then stirred the rest.

"But he set the whole thing up and you walked out on him!"

Alicia scraped the bottom of her carton. Georgia was supposed to be taking her part, not defending Tony. "He knows why I left," she grumbled.

"Maybe he doesn't. And, Alicia, sugar," Georgia continued delicately, "maybe you overestimated his feelings."

"Oh, please! He can't go around kissing women the way he kissed me and expect them to ignore it."

"So how does Mr. Domenico kiss?" Georgia asked slyly.

"Oh, Georgia . . . we first kissed in the moonlight and he told me he'd never again look at the moon without thinking of me."

"Tony said that? *Our* Tony?"

"*My* Tony."

"He's not going to be your Tony if you don't turn around and get back to Roperville and fight for him." As Georgia spoke, one of the twins kicked and toppled the ice-cream carton she'd balanced on her stomach.

Alicia rescued it. "Are you going to eat this? It's a dairy product. Very healthy for pregnant women."

"I'm full. There's not much room these days." Georgia shifted to her side. "If you leave now, you can be in east Texas by one o'clock."

"I don't have time to go back," Alicia said around a mouthful of Georgia's ice cream. This second pint didn't taste as good as the first. "I'm starting postproduction on 'A Hartson Flowers Valentine'."

"No, you're avoiding Tony."

"And I will continue to avoid him," Alicia vowed. "I've had practice. In fact, he's mentioned selling us to the networks." She tilted up her chin. "I hope he does. Then I'll never have to see him again."

Georgia handed her a tissue. "Your tears are dripping into the ice cream."

The phone rang. Georgia answered it, and by her expression, Alicia knew it was Tony.

Thursday dawned gray and drippy, which precisely matched Tony's mood.

Alicia might as well have disappeared off the face of the earth. He'd called everyone—Georgia twice, but she'd said she hadn't heard from Alicia. Tony didn't know whether he believed her or not. He almost told her what he had planned, then didn't.

He had to leave for the stadium now. Staring at the telephone, he gave into a last impulse and called Georgia once more.

"Hello?" Her drawl was reassuringly familiar.

"Georgia, it's Tony again. Look, I'm not going to ask you if you've heard from Alicia. But if you do, just tell her I need her."

"For the competition segment?"

That, too. "Yeah." His voice was rough.

There was a silence. "You sound exhausted."

"I haven't slept all night."

"You haven't slept all night," Georgia repeated.

"And I would like for my producer to be here and produce!" Tony snapped, then apologized. "Sorry."

"That's all right. I understand. You depended on Alicia and she let you down."

"Not really. She did tape some—"

"It's not like her to quit before the job is finished. Very unprofessional."

"I realize her first priority is the Valentine special." He closed his eyes and continued in a quiet voice. "I just want to make sure she's okay."

"I'm sure she's fine. I'll give her your message when she checks in with me."

"Thanks, Georgia." He'd hung up the phone and was staring at it when it rang again. "Hello?" It had to be Alicia.

"Mr. Domenico?"

Tony sagged. "Yes?"

"This is Kwik Print. Are you going to pick up the cards you ordered, or should I deliver them to the stadium?"

The pink cards for his proposal to Alicia. He didn't need them now and he briefly considered calling the whole thing off. But people had gone out of their way for him. Better to continue and tell them things didn't work out later. "Send the cards to the stadium. Thanks."

This afternoon, just after the noon break, he was proposing to Alicia. She wouldn't see it, but somewhere, he hoped that another man was ready to propose to his Alicia and could use the help.

"*Unprofessional*?" Alicia glared.

"I call 'em like I see 'em," Georgia said.

"Unprofessional." Alicia stood and cleared away the ice cream. "I am *never* unprofessional." She stuffed the debris into the trash. "I am known for my professionalism. Ask anybody in the industry and they'll tell you Alicia Hartson is a *professional*."

Georgia laced her fingers over her stomach. "I think I'll ask Tony."

Alicia gritted her teeth and breathed heavily. "That was low. That was *really* low, Georgia." Snatching up her purse, she marched from the room.

"But really effective," Georgia murmured to herself. She smiled. "I am *so* good."

After an hour on site, Tony missed Alicia, the producer, as much as he missed her as a person. Trying

to coordinate both camera teams, as well as over-
seeing each and every detail of his larger-than-life
proposal, was high-octane stress. Knowing it was
all for nothing was torture.

A voice sounded on the van radio. "Tony?" The
speaker was one of the college students he'd hired
to pull this off.

Wearily, Tony picked up the microphone.
"Yes?"

"Where's the food for the pigeons?"

Tony rested his head on the steering wheel. They
were supposed to be doves. He'd wanted hundreds
of white doves. What he got were a couple of dozen
white pigeons because the doves had had their wings
clipped and couldn't fly. From a distance, he'd
hoped the effect would be the same. "I hadn't
planned to feed them. Where's the handler?"

"I don't know."

"Perhaps," Tony said in a careful voice, "you
could locate him?"

"Okay."

Tony stared sightlessly out the van's windshield
at the group performing below him on the field.
With a precision that spoke of long practice, they
crisscrossed the field in lines, diamonds and circles.
The flag corps was fighting against the wind gusts
and two band members had lost their hats.

Tony had chosen this spot because it was on the
upper rim at the end of the field, behind the
goalpost. From this vantage point, both sides of
the stadium were visible, as was the scoreboard and
the field.

Jake was here and Tony's cameraman was in the
announcer/press box. Tony was coordinating feed

from both cameras. If Alicia were here, he'd see that she joined him on the hill right before the Louisiana College Lions took the field. Together, they would watch.

The Lions would position themselves on the sidelines, but instead of marching onto the field, the trumpets would blow a fanfare. That was the signal for the audience in sections C, D, E and F to hold up the cards they'd been given. Assuming everyone sat where he was supposed to and no one was in line at either the rest rooms or the concession stand, the pink cards would spell out in solid black letters, "WILL YOU MARRY ME, ALICIA?" The scoreboard would blink in patterns of hearts and wedding bells. When Alicia said yes, Tony would radio the board operator, who'd then flash the message to the spectators, which would signal the release of the pigeons and thousands of pink, heart-shaped balloons.

Jake would turn the camera on them and their happy faces would appear on the giant field television screen. And Alicia would never again be impressed by any other proposal "Hartson Flowers" taped.

But Alicia wasn't here.

And there were just four more colleges to compete before the Lions.

Tony hadn't confided in the crew, though the sound tech was sitting in the back of the van and must have heard not only the pigeon conversation, but the pink-card-and-balloon conversations. The guys were smart. They'd be able to figure it out.

"If anyone calls for me, I'll be outside," Tony told the tech.

Late January was a funny time of year in this part of Texas. Cold air from the north battled warm fronts from the Gulf of Mexico resulting in rapid weather changes. The cold air he and Alicia had endured on the west Texas shoot had blown across Texas to reach Roperville and had encountered the warm, moist air resulting in the scattered showers that had interrupted today's competition twice already.

All morning long, the sky had spit at him. *Life* had spit at him.

Tony should have grabbed Alicia when he had the chance.

The next band took the field. And the next.

A light rain began to fall.

"Great," he muttered and helped Jake cover the camera.

Flashes of pink caught Tony's eye as several people used his cards to cover their heads.

The rain fell harder.

"Tony?"

He stared at Jake.

Jake gestured to the field. "We've got plenty of footage, man."

"Yeah." Tony turned up the collar on his jacket. He could smell the faint scent of Alicia's perfume. "Go ahead and pack up," he told the cameraman.

Jake looked as though he was about to say something, then thought better of it and hauled the camera and tripod back to the van.

The performing group valiantly continued, but the flags no longer fluttered and the feather head-pieces on the band's hats had turned into sodden lumps. More than one marcher slipped on the artificial turf.

Spectators sought shelter. Some of the pink cards flew onto the field. Loud whistles shrilled from the drum major and the band ran off the field.

"The Southwest Regional Marching Band and Flag Corps Competition has been postponed due to inclement weather," echoed the stadium loudspeakers. "The Arkansas State Armadillos will be allowed to repeat their presentation. Please see that a representative from each group yet to perform stays in touch with competition officials. We will advise you of the revised performing schedule as soon as weather permits."

A white bird flew around the stadium. One of the pigeons must have escaped. Instead of hearts and wedding bells, the stadium scoreboard flashed, "Competition postponed." Pink cards littered the seats and concrete stairs.

And still Tony stood in the rain.

"Hey, man, you coming?" Jake and the sound tech, wearing ugly yellow ponchos, appeared beside him.

"I'm not ready to leave yet, we've got—"

"We're not leaving!" the sound tech interrupted.

"We're headed for the concession stand," Jake clarified. "They're going to be unloading food for next to nothing. All those hot dogs and nachos can't be saved. We've got to get there before the college kids clean them out!"

Tony sent them off with a wave.

He didn't feel like eating. Burying his nose in his jacket collar, he inhaled, breathing in the memory of Alicia.

Even if she'd been here, his proposal would have been a disaster. Romance just wasn't worth the effort.

The custodial staff had begun to clear away the trash. Tony stared as they scooped the pink cards along with empty cups and cardboard food containers into large plastic bags.

Trash. What would have been the most romantic proposal in the world had been reduced to soggy trash.

A vehicle pulled up behind him. He ignored it. "Mr. Domenico?"

Reluctantly turning his head, he saw a stadium truck.

The driver jerked a thumb toward the back. "We've got your balloons. Sorry, but they're in the way. Where do you want them?"

He didn't want them. He didn't care if he ever saw another balloon, a heart or the color pink again. "Unload them by the van and I'll deal with them later."

The men wrestled with three gigantic nets filled with two thousand pink, helium-filled, heart-shaped balloons. The bags were attached to huge, doughnut-shaped weights. Tony shook his head. The balloons would never fit in the van. He'd have to cut them loose and return the weights to the rental agency.

Leaning against the chain-link fence, he raised his face to the sky and let the rain pelt him. The stadium truck drove off and he was alone.

His one grand romantic gesture was a complete failure. When Alicia had suggested a celebration, it would have been completely natural to say, "If you'll marry me, then we'll have even more to celebrate.'' Then they would have been engaged and he wouldn't be standing out here in the rain wondering if she'd ever speak to him again.

Rain dribbled into the neck of his jacket and Tony decided to move, not because he particularly wanted to get out of the rain, but because he was afraid the moisture would obliterate the last traces of Alicia's perfume.

Moving to the shelter of the ticket gate, he sat in a metal folding chair and watched stadium personnel clear away the stray pink cards. He probably should lend a hand since he was the cause of the extra trash.

A car door slammed and footsteps crunched over the gravel. Tony sighed. He'd wondered how long it would be before the pigeon handler found him.

"Tony?" It was a female voice.

"Alicia!" She was there. She'd come back. Tony could only stare as she picked her way through the puddles.

"You're wet." Alicia joined him under the ticket gate overhang and closed her umbrella.

"It's raining." That wasn't what he'd wanted to say.

"I know." She sighed and her breath puffed a white cloud in the cool air. "I apologize for leaving you to tape this segment by yourself. I shouldn't have." She shivered. Her nose was pink. "It was...unprofessional of me."

Tony ignored her apology. "You're cold." He unzipped his jacket and held out his arms. "Come here."

She glanced at him, then concentrated on shaking the dripping umbrella. "I don't think that's wise."

A raindrop slid down the side of his neck. "I don't care if it's wise or not." He stepped closer. "I need to hold you."

Her lip trembled and she launched herself at him. "Not as much as I need to be held," she said, circling his waist under the jacket.

"Alicia." Tony closed his arms around her, holding her close even after her shivering stopped. "I love you."

"You're just saying that because you feel sorry for me." The words were muffled against his chest.

"I'm saying that because I love you." He kissed the top of her head because that was the only part of her he could reach.

She pulled back to look up at him. "Then why didn't you let me speak the other day? You must have known how I felt."

He touched his forehead to hers. "I didn't want you to spoil your proposal."

"What proposal?" She searched his face, her eyes wide.

Tony waved his arm. "I had brass bands. I had this entire stadium full of people...but I didn't have you." Looking down at her, he smiled crookedly. "I blew it. I'm sorry."

"Tony..." She sighed his name and her expression softened. "I don't need brass bands or people or cameras or anything but you. I love you. That's why I tried to propose to you. I wanted you to see that I could do without all that 'romantic fluff' as you call it."

She sounded as though she meant it. "But I wanted that romantic fluff for you."

"And I adore you for it."

She was looking at him with such love that Tony couldn't wait. There, alone in the rain, he felt the words well out of his heart. "Will you marry me, Alicia?"

Tears formed in her eyes. "Yes," she whispered and trembled.

Joy squeezed his heart as he kissed her. "I wanted this to be so romantic for you. Just like in your dreams."

"It *is* romantic." She raised her arm. "Look. Goose bumps."

As Tony bent his head, intending to kiss each and every one of those goose bumps, he stopped and a grin split his face. "Come with me." Linking her fingers with his, he pulled her from beneath their shelter and ran with her out into the open.

"Wait right here." Cupping his mouth with his hands, he shouted to the disinterested custodial staff, "She said yes! Alicia Hartson is going to marry Tony Domenico!"

"Tony!" Laughing, Alicia hid her face against him. "We can tell the world later."

"Oh, we will." Tony dropped one last kiss on her lips before jogging to the van. "Watch!"

And then he released all two thousand pink hearts and sent them floating into the sky, just for her.

EPILOGUE

"HAPPY Valentine's Day! This is Alicia Hartson here at Park Wood Hospital in Houston, Texas, where my partner, Georgia Flowers, has just given birth to twins! Yes, on Valentine's Day!" Alicia beamed into the camera. "Her twin girls were born this morning and we thought pictures of the new mother and her daughters would be just the thing to end our annual Valentine to our viewers."

Alicia held her smile until Tony signaled a cut.

"Is Georgia ready yet?" she asked. "She's been in makeup for an hour."

"Just about," Tony answered. "I'm amazed. I can't believe the woman gave birth only this morning."

"Great timing, wasn't it?" Alicia grinned. "Though the babies were a month early, they're a good size." Shifting gears, she said, "We need forty-five seconds and we'll run the closing credits on top instead of using the balloon footage."

"You don't think Susie and Philip will mind?"

Alicia was scribbling instructions. "Susie's just thrilled we were able to fit in any of their proposal. Four proposals in a half-hour show was a little tight."

"You're a softie."

Tony rubbed her shoulders and Alicia smiled up at him before standing on her tiptoes to see into Georgia's room. "They're doing her lips. Georgia always does lips last.'' Alicia signaled Jake. ''We tape in five.''

Tony checked his watch. ''That'll give us plenty of time to edit and transmit the new ending to the stations broadcasting your special tonight. And then it's off to my parents.''

Alicia put her hand on her middle. ''Your mother promised me lasagna tonight. Yum.''

''My mother would cook anything for you.''

''And I will let her.''

They both laughed.

''I haven't properly thanked you for whatever it was that you said to Peter.'' Tony raised his eyebrows.

Alicia hadn't told him much of her conversation with his brother-in-law because she was afraid he'd think she was meddling. And after all, she *was* meddling. ''Basically, I pointed out that his poetry was shallow—I was gentle—because he'd been writing about life from the sidelines. He hadn't experienced the everyday struggle of man versus the world. He'd only observed others struggling. And his poetry reflected this lack of experience. It didn't ring true to those who worked hard day after day. And—'' she looked down at her hands ''—I pointed out the perfect example right in his own home with Thea and the kids.''

''Is *that* why Thea is staying in your apartment?''

Alicia nodded. ''And because she needs a break. Peter wanted to see what the struggle of the single mother is all about. Today was his third day. He made your mom promise not to help him, and according to Thea, she hasn't.''

Tony shook his head. "I can't believe this. And the European trip?"

Alicia shrugged. "Maybe for their tenth anniversary."

"You are amazing and I love you." He kissed her.

"Remind me to touch up my lipstick," Alicia said, and kissed him back. "Which, unfortunately, I should do right now."

"Wait a minute." Tony caught Alicia's hand. "Jake?" He twirled his finger for Jake to tape.

"What's he taping?" Alicia asked.

"This." Smiling, Tony reached into his pocket, withdrew a red velvet ring box and flipped it open.

"Tony!" Alicia clasped her hands over her mouth, just as nearly every other bride had done. "It's a heart-shaped diamond!"

He slipped it onto her finger. "Happy Valentine's Day."

"Oh, Tony." She stared at the ring, tears blurring the sparkle. "When I look at it, it'll seem like every day is Valentine's Day."

He drew her close. "Because with you, every day *is* Valentine's Day."

Harlequin Romance ®

brings you

SIMPLY THE BEST

Authors you'll treasure, books you'll want to keep!

Harlequin Romance books just keep getting better and better...and we're delighted to welcome you to our **Simply the Best** showcase for 1997, highlighting a special author each month!

Watch for:

#3448 GETTING OVER HARRY
by Renee Roszel

Emily has been jilted at the altar, and her best friend, Meg, convinces her to take a holiday to get over it. But Emily refuses to be persuaded that the best cure for a broken heart is another romance. Enter Lyon Gallant on the scene: he's rich, he's cute—and he wants Emily!

"Renee Roszel heats up your reading pleasure."
—*Romantic Times*

"Fast moving and entertaining, sparkling to the very end!" —*Affaire de Coeur* on *Dare to Kiss a Cowboy*

"Ms Roszel produces exciting characters and dialogue that packs a punch." —*Rendezvous*

Available in March wherever
Harlequin books are sold.

 **HARLEQUIN®**

Don't miss these Harlequin favorites by some of our most
distinguished authors!
And now, you can receive a discount by ordering two or more titles!

HT#25645	THREE GROOMS AND A WIFE by JoAnn Ross	$3.25 U.S. $3.75 CAN.	☐
HT#25647	NOT THIS GUY by Glenda Sanders	$3.25 U.S. $3.75 CAN.	☐
HP#11725	THE WRONG KIND OF WIFE by Roberta Leigh	$3.25 U.S. $3.75 CAN.	☐
HP#11755	TIGER EYES by Robyn Donald	$3.25 U.S. $3.75 CAN.	☐
HR#03416	A WIFE IN WAITING by Jessica Steele	$3.25 U.S. $3.75 CAN.	☐
HR#03419	KIT AND THE COWBOY by Rebecca Winters	$3.25 U.S. $3.75 CAN.	☐
HS#70622	KIM & THE COWBOY by Margot Dalton	$3.50 U.S. $3.99 CAN.	☐
HS#70642	MONDAY'S CHILD by Janice Kaiser	$3.75 U.S. $4.25 CAN.	☐
HI#22342	BABY VS. THE BAR by M.J. Rodgers	$3.50 U.S. $3.99 CAN.	☐
HI#22382	SEE ME IN YOUR DREAMS by Patricia Rosemoor	$3.75 U.S. $4.25 CAN.	☐
HAR#16538	KISSED BY THE SEA by Rebecca Flanders	$3.50 U.S. $3.99 CAN.	☐
HAR#16603	MOMMY ON BOARD by Muriel Jensen	$3.50 U.S. $3.99 CAN.	☐
HH#28885	DESERT ROGUE by Erine Yorke	$4.50 U.S. $4.99 CAN.	☐
HH#28911	THE NORMAN'S HEART by Margaret Moore	$4.50 U.S. $4.99 CAN.	☐

(limited quantities available on certain titles)

	AMOUNT	$
DEDUCT:	10% DISCOUNT FOR 2+ BOOKS	$
ADD:	POSTAGE & HANDLING	$
	($1.00 for one book, 50¢ for each additional)	
	APPLICABLE TAXES*	$_____
	TOTAL PAYABLE	$_____
	(check or money order—please do not send cash)	

To order, complete this form and send it, along with a check or money order for the
total above, payable to Harlequin Books, to: **In the U.S.:** 3010 Walden Avenue,
P.O. Box 9047, Buffalo, NY 14269-9047; **In Canada:** P.O. Box 613, Fort Erie, Ontario,
L2A 5X3.

Name: _____

Address: _____ City: _____

State/Prov.: _____ Zip/Postal Code: _____

*New York residents remit applicable sales taxes.
 Canadian residents remit applicable GST and provincial taxes.
Look us up on-line at: http://www.romance.net

HBACK-JM4